To Terri,
Enjoy Fox!

FOX

THE PLAYER

Nana Malone

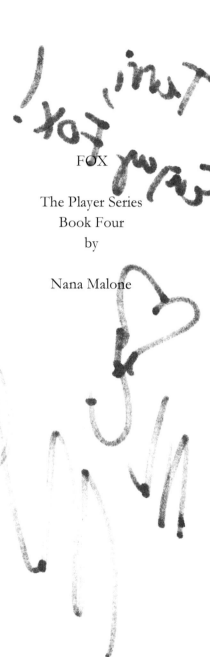

FOX

The Player Series
Book Four
by

Nana Malone

FOX
COPYRIGHT 2017 BY NANA MALONE

Cover Art by Jena Brignola
Edited by Tanya Saari
Proof Editing Angie Ramey

Published in the United States of America

Dedication

To *The Mighty Ducks* for developing my unholy love for sports movies.

Chapter One

Fox Coulter fidgeted on his skates, shifting his weight from one foot to the other. He tapped the toe of his left skate with the oversized blade of his goalie's stick.

Two other goalies stood on either side of him as the coaches for the New York Brawlers deliberated over which of them they'd call up to fill the backup position for the upcoming season. He barely resisted the urge to shout, "Pick me!" Their former backup had been a free agent and signed with Dallas a week after the end of the previous season.

Fox sized up the guys on either side of him as best he could without looking at them or acknowledging their presence. It was all part of the game. On his right was Henri Jacobson. He had come to the United States to play just a year earlier when he was seventeen, having already been on one of Sweden's professional teams for two years. On his left was Bobby Jones. He'd just graduated high school and had a scholarship to Boston College waiting for him if the Brawlers didn't choose him.

Fox was twenty-one and had been kicking around the minor league farm system since his own high school graduation three years earlier. He had been offered a place on the hockey team at several colleges. Some had even offered him a little scholarship money, but he'd turned them all down, opting for playing semi-professionally right off the bat.

He'd never been academically inclined, and there was nothing he wanted to do except play hockey, so college seemed like a waste of time.

Now he wondered if he'd made a mistake. He'd underestimated how difficult it would be for him to distinguish himself as a goalie. It wasn't a position with a lot of turnover or flexibility like forwards or defensemen. Most teams had their main goalie and a backup — *maybe* two — who got ice time for one game in four or five. Fox had thought he'd play one season in the farm system before his call came, maybe even less. But it had been three years and still he hadn't been called up. Instead, he was starting to see players younger than him getting offered contracts. True, few of them were goalies, but it still made him feel older than he thought it should. Fuck, had he screwed up his life?

When he looked at his older brothers, or hell, at his sister Echo, and saw where they were with their careers, he felt like he was a lost cause. The Coulter who had failed.

Bryce had several major doubles tennis titles

under his belt with his wife, Tami, and was famous for the comeback he'd made after a serious injury. Dax had just signed a contract extension with Jacksonville's pro football franchise, and the team was continuing to improve under their new coaches. They had made it all the way to the AFC Championship last season before getting knocked out by the Broncos on their way to the Superbowl. Echo was an Olympic silver medalist in track, and had started transitioning into an entrepreneur and fashion designer. Shit, even his little brother Gage was more successful with his scholarship to San Diego University and a prominent placement on their basketball team. The commentators who were already hyping next spring's March Madness brackets were speculating that he might even be better than their father Brent, who was a legend in his own right. Hell, his season hadn't even started yet.

The coaches deliberated out of earshot, and Fox began to feel the cold radiating off the ice, even under the layers of padding. He started going over each mistake he'd made during the skills demonstrations they'd run through.

The scrimmages had gone well enough. Fox knew he was solid when there were five men on the ice working with him. They had his back and were counting on him to have theirs as well. He was quick to pass the puck when he got it in the trapezoid behind the net and made it back to block the net easily. There were quite a few saves he'd made that had clearly impressed them. The team had impressed *him* as well. Fuck, he wanted this. But there had also been more than a few missed saves that he *should* have had; basic fake-outs he'd fallen for, and would continue to beat himself up over. Penalties were his biggest weakness. One-on-one, as players lined up to take unimpeded shots on him in practice, he was able to stop about half of them. In a shoot-out situation, his numbers dropped by more than half. And he hadn't done any better than that during the scrimmages the coaches had orchestrated.

If he was honest with himself, he knew what was coming, but he still tried to steel himself against the blow. Henri had done better than him, and his experience in Europe carried more weight than the Coulter name and legacy in this situation. His father's and grandfather's connections didn't extend into the hockey world.

Fox had always been the odd one out in his choice of sport. The lone child of winter while his siblings had all played in the warmth of summer — or at least indoor warmth. But he loved working up a sweat to combat the chill of the rink.

Of his brothers, he was the only one who had taken to a defensive position. Tennis required a bit of both, but with Tami at Bryce's side, the pressure and responsibility were halved. Dax and Gage both enjoyed the glory of being the one scoring points for their team.

Fox bore the weight of the goals scored against his. If the other team scored, it was his fault because he was the last line of defense. He had little control over his teammates' success in scoring, but he was the one between the pipes, making sure that whatever they did score truly counted.

The coaches emerged from the bench area and approached Bobby first, thanked him for showing them what he could do and wished him luck at BC. They assured him that they'd be keeping an eye on his college career, and that they were sure they wouldn't be alone in that. Then the eighteen-year-old skated off the ice, leaving just Fox and Henri with the coaches.

Fox took a deep breath and puffed up his chest, praying their eyes would go to the younger man at his right.

They looked at him. *Fuck.*

"Fox, you're a talented and knowledgeable goalie. The team you're with now is very lucky to have you," Coach Tremblay began. "This was an incredibly tough decision to have to make, and we wish we could extend an offer to both of you. But given the schedule we're facing and the competition in our conference, we're going to have to leave you where you are for the time being."

Coach Tremblay indicated for Fox to follow him a short distance away while his assistant coach tried to explain what was going on to Henri, who was still working on his English. Fox's pads suddenly felt like they weighed five hundred pounds, but he moved his legs and leaned on the stick to keep himself upright as Coach Tremblay continued.

"We're going to be keeping an eye on your numbers during this season, and if your clinch numbers improve a bit more, I promise you we'll be paying you another visit. It's just that we're anticipating a tough race in the conference to make the play-offs. The Rajun Cajuns are going to be tough to beat. We're going to need those ties to be overtime wins and…it's just not your strongest area. But improve there and in penalty kill goals, and we won't be the only team showing an interest in you for long."

Fox forced his mouth to move. "Thank you, sir," he managed to say as they reached the boards, and Coach Tremblay held out a hand for Fox to shake. Moving his stick and tucking his gloved hand under his other arm, he pulled his hand free to shake the coach's before turning and heading down to the locker room. He didn't let himself sag until he was safely inside.

Bobby had already cleared out by the time he got there, so he had the place to himself. Thank fuck. They'd held the goalies for the end, of course, so the other players had gone home to celebrate or commiserate.

Fox checked the messages on his phone, knowing there would be texts from his friends for him to join them. Most of them had been through the process enough times that they were familiar with the disappointment. Or they'd already had their brief time in the big leagues and were on their way down again because of injuries or age.

Many had simply gone home to their wives and children, but they weren't the teammates he was closest to. Most of his closest friends had been picked up to play the preseason with the team, and while he desperately wanted a drink, he wasn't in the mood to drink with any of them. He didn't want their pity or their reassurances. Not this time.

And he wasn't ready to go home. It hadn't been the same since Echo moved out some months before. He'd been crashing with his teammates more often than not. His trust fund had kicked in on his twenty-first birthday, and unlike the rest of his siblings, he had actually started dipping into it regularly. They all had other sources of income to fall back on; endorsements, spokesperson gigs, and paid appearances. And then there was Echo, who was developing her own athletic wear line.

He needed to move out. And while his minor league salary wasn't enough for the kind of place he wanted, his trust fund would make up the difference…if he let it. He didn't want to rely on that money. Not in that way. It was tantamount to admitting failure. And he wasn't ready to throw in the towel just yet. Or admit that to anyone. Especially not his family. He was the only Coulter to never reach his full potential. Congratulations to him.

***

Sasha Tenison knew better than to answer the phone when assholes called, but this particular asshole couldn't be avoided. She answered on the third ring. "Hi dad."

"Where are you? I called your office and was told you weren't there."

She bit her bottom lip to keep from groaning. She hated it when he checked up on her. It was as if he thought she was a child who needed his protection, or worse, his berating.

"I'm just waiting to see a friend. I'll be headed back to the office in a little bit," she replied with a sigh. She shouldn't have answered. She didn't have the patience for this conversation right now.

"Why you insist on working there is beyond me. It's like I never taught you better," he scolded.

It was times like this when she has truly hated him. Ever since her mother left, Sasha had been her father's special project. The man seriously needed his own hobbies.

"Dad, we've been through this. This is what I want to do."

"We both know you're not going to listen to me anyway. When have you ever done that? Exhibit A: that loser you're dating."

This was such a tired conversation. They'd had it a million times, and nothing was ever going to change. Her father was an old-school misogynist who believed that the only place for a woman was in the kitchen, barefoot and pregnant.

How her mother had dealt with him for so long, Sasha had no idea. After all, her mother was a traditional debutante. She was the whole package. But eventually, the pressure of having to be the 'perfect athlete's wife' had gotten to her, and she'd left when Sasha was eight years old. At this point, Sasha understood why her mother had left and didn't blame her. What she didn't understand was why her mother left *her* behind. *Whatever, it's water under the bridge now.*

The problem this time, though, was that her father was right about her loser boyfriend. Ryan was a total dipshit. She knew it. His jealousy had gotten out of control lately. She needed to do something about it, but right now she was in avoidance mode.

You know how, you're just too lazy and tired.

Man, was she tired. Between her internship at TVN television network, her job at the restaurant, and her schoolwork, she didn't have time to breathe. Let alone, cater to her boyfriend's every whim. Or her father's, for that matter, even though her father was right. Ryan was convenient and available. He'd long outlived his welcome, but she was too exhausted to make any changes.

Yeah, like that's a good reason.

"Dad, you don't have to tell me how you feel about him every time we talk. I already know."

But her father was no longer listening. "What I find exasperating, is that you refuse to do anything about it. Even when you have better prospects. Fox

Coulter has been sniffing around since you guys were kids, and you still haven't pulled the trigger on that. You're missing out on a prime opportunity you won't have forever. God knows I'm not giving you a trust fund or college fund. You have to leverage what you have, because nothing else is coming for you."

As if there is a college or trust fund to be had. The whole world knew he'd squandered the fortune given to him by her grandfather. He'd also squandered what he had earned from his own football career. Although, what he earned hadn't gone far — her father liked to spend as though there was an endless pool of cash coming his way. And a lifetime of injuries had kept him from playing again.

"I know, Dad. Listen, I have to go. I'm waiting on Fox."

"You got that boy on a hook. You better get yourself a piece of that Coulter money, because I'm not gonna take care of you."

"Yeah, I got that," she bit out.

She hung up the phone and shoved it back into her pocket. She didn't want to think about her father. She hardly ever saw him, but she couldn't help but answer when he called because the guilt ate away at her. If she didn't answer the phone, then who would? Lord knew the man didn't have anyone. And as much as she disliked him, he was still her father. Her sense of obligation was usually what got her into trouble. That's why she had been with Ryan for this long.

She set those thoughts aside. She wasn't here for either of them. Right now, she was here for Fox. She hoped and prayed that he had made it this time. She knew how it killed him to get this close but not quite make it. He'd be devastated, and she never knew how to help.

Fox was good. Really, really good. Watching him skate and play was like a revelation. Everyone from his family to sports enthusiasts said it and had high hopes for him. Fox's biggest obstacle was that he always managed to psych himself out, always getting too much into his own head. She knew that better than anyone because she had been his best friend for the past ten years. This time, she prayed he would get everything he had ever dreamt of.

He worked harder than anyone she knew, even in high school. He would always be on the ice before anyone else, practicing long before he had to be there. There was nothing Fox wanted more than to be on the ice.

She prayed hard that this time, he would get his dream. Simply because it killed her to watch him beat himself up when shit didn't go his way.

When the side doors opened to the arena, she watched as one of the biggest men she'd ever seen lumbered out with a bag on his shoulder. No denying it, this guy was one of the players. One by one, she watched as huge tree trunks of men filed out. She prayed that he wouldn't come out of the door next.

She looked at the sign she had brought, it was their thing. One side said, *Congratulations, Let's Get Drunk*. And the other side was the dreaded *other*. She hoped she wouldn't have to flip her sign over.

The door opened once more, and Sasha silently pleaded for it not to be Fox. She knew the longer he was in there, the better the news was. Even if the San Diego sun wasn't shining brightly in the sky making his numerous tattoos stand out, she'd recognize his build. Still, Sasha held onto her hope. She held up her sign of *Congratulations, Let's Get Drunk!* with a bright smile on her face and continued her silent prayer.

Please, please, please God. Please, please, please let him have made it.

As he approached, she knew that his dreams weren't coming true today. No one was hearing her prayers. But she refused to give up on him.

She held her sign high and yelled, "So, where're we drinkin', superstar?"

Fox shook his head. "We're not. They went with Henri."

Sasha's heart sank. She wanted to run up to him, cradle him in her arms, and say that everything was going to be okay. She knew better than to do that, though. Instead, she kept her smile in place and turned her sign over to the side that said, *Fuck Them, Let's Go Drink.*

"I see you changed it." Behind the sorrow, she saw a glimmer of humor. Her Fox was in there somewhere.

She *had* changed up the sign. He'd been going on more and more tryouts, just to come home disappointed each time. She didn't want to seem predictable, so she kept trying to come up with one that would make him laugh.

"Well, I can't let you figure me out. You don't want me to get boring, do you?"

Fox shook his head, "Thanks Sash, but I kinda want to be on my own tonight."

She could see the shadow pressing on his shoulders. "Look, it'll happen, Fox. Just believe me, I'm never wrong."

He gave her a weary smile, "I know. Still, I'm just gonna head on out."

When he got like this, there wasn't much she could do except wait for him to come around. "I hear you. But obviously, you know, if you need to talk—" she stopped. *He doesn't want my pity.*

"I know."

"You know, you still haven't seen my new place. You could drop by with a bottle of wine, or something."

A smile tipped his lips. "Yeah, I got you, Sash. Call you later."

Sasha could only watch as Fox lumbered to his car. She hoped he would be ok. She wasn't sure how much longer she could watch the disappointment sink into him. She hoped that something happened for him soon. He deserved it.

Without Fox, her choices were to either go home or to the office. Before she even pondered her options, she knew where she was going. The office, because the longer she could put off the impending confrontation with Ryan, the better.

Chapter Two

Sasha could only avoid going home for so long. It was after 8 o'clock, and there was barely anyone on the news floor. She loved her internship at TVN and she knew how lucky she was to have it. So many other students had been declined. She still wasn't sure how she got accepted, but she was making the most of it.

Her mentor, Ida Bailey, spotted her at her desk. "Hey Sasha, I'm glad to still find you here. Do you have a sec to talk about your proposal?"

Sasha loved that Ida hadn't questioned her about being there so late. Long after most of the other interns and experienced news crew had cleared out, Sasha could usually be found at her desk.

"Sure," Sasha replied, feeling pleased.

"So far, what I've seen looks great. Let's talk in more detail in the morning, okay? I want you to come prepped with the sources you want to use, and the research you've already compiled. At this point, though, I'm very satisfied. You could really spread your wings, here. Make an impact."

"I certainly hope so."

"Well then, you should head on out for the night. Don't you have a boyfriend to go home to?"

The question made Sasha's gut curl in on itself. "Uh, yeah, I was just packing up my things." Maybe she could track Fox down and help him drown his sorrows. Right now, that was a far more appealing prospect than going home. Sasha checked the clock again; it was 8:30. She couldn't avoid it forever, but right now she had work to do. That story proposal was her ticket to her future.

***

Shit, he was drunk. At this point, Fox was no longer looking at the line items on his tab. The more he drank, the more he kicked himself for not having chosen the college track. He was twenty-one. He would have been in his junior or senior year by now. College hockey wasn't as nationally prominent as college football or basketball, but he would have had broader exposure. Not to mention an education that would have left him with a degree to fall back on.

As it was, he would only be able to stick it out a few more years in the minor leagues before all chance at the majors would vanish. How long had it been since any of the teams had called up anyone over the age of twenty-five who wasn't just playing in the minors as part of an injury-recovery stint?

There were only four years between him and the point at which he'd effectively be washed up.

And worse than a has-been, he'd be a never-has-been-*and*-never-will-be. After twenty-five, how many years would he even be allowed to remain in the minor leagues? He'd need to find something else to do.

As if there *were* anything for him outside of playing hockey. If he didn't make it or come up with an alternative plan, he'd have to cave and rely on his trust fund for everything until he could figure things out. There wasn't enough money in his trust fund for him to live off of it indefinitely. Even the Coulter name didn't come with unlimited funds. The millions would run out eventually. *Then what will you do?*

So far his father hadn't extended an offer for him to work for Legacy Sports, the family's sports equipment retail company. Bryce had been invited following his knee injury, but had vehemently rebelled against being encouraged in that direction. Echo had spent time working for the company, coordinating their charity efforts, before she, too, quit with an unexpected flourish. Dax hadn't done anything in the company's administration, but the store had been able to capitalize on his popularity as an NFL player.

What did it say that his father hadn't even bothered to ask him about joining the company and keeping things in the family? Not that he would accept if the old man ever *did* make such an offer. He had zero interest in being stuck in a boardroom or learning what to do about missed shipments, vendor relations, or managing any sort of staff.

But given his father's recent health concerns, there had been more talk about the company's future should he need to take time off or retire altogether. And to the best of Fox's knowledge, his name was never a part of any discussion.

The answers he came up with only drove him to drink more.

If things didn't change quickly, he'd be up a creek with no paddle. It might be time to sit down with his unofficial career consultant, *Sasha*.

He smiled to himself. Sasha Tenison had been as much a fixture in his life as hockey was. Their grandfathers had played football together, and their families had been close ever since. She'd been a whiz in school and had saved his academic ass more than once. Although she liked to point out he understood things *best* when he read the assignments on time. He just didn't have the time or inclination for those kinds of homework assignments. Hockey practices and games held most of his focus.

It was all well and good for Sasha. She'd

wanted to be in journalism and had been one of the anchors for their high school's morning announcements. She'd even been on local San Diego television.

They'd been like oil and water, but as thick as thieves in spite of that fact. No matter what, she was always there for him. And he was there for her. It's just how it was. Things had been strained lately because of her boyfriend, but the guy was a douche and Fox was just waiting for the day he needed to turn up at her place with wine, a tub of ice-cream, and cheesy sci-fi movies. Ryan was temporary; *he* was forever.

The evening had long ago reached a point where the bartender asked for his car keys, leaving him with limited mobility. He could call a cab, but imagining the look on his parents' faces when he rolled home lacked a certain appeal.

His friends would be equally shitfaced by this time, and had likely figured out that he wouldn't be joining them as the preseason began. Depending on how much they had drunk, they would either be overly sympathetic and reassuring or they would give him a good ribbing over the whole thing. He wasn't sufficiently in enough control of his limbs to feel confident of being able to withstand either treatment without taking a swing at someone.

It took a few minutes for Fox to figure out if he knew of anyone else in the area who might be willing to let him crash on their couch until he sobered up. Maybe he just had Sasha on his mind, but a part of him wanted to see her. *Because you're a glutton for punishment.* No. They were friends. It was just Sasha. They'd been friends forever. He sucked at trying to convince himself he didn't have it bad for her. Usually, he didn't care too much who she dated. But this last asshole — it required all of his strength not to flatten the dude.

His fingers refused to cooperate as he navigated his controls to his favorites on his contact list. She didn't answer, but he could find her place. It wasn't far. He'd just never done it wasted before. But likely that was because she'd moved there only two months ago. A drunken visit was inevitable. *But what would Ryan think?* Shit. Dude was not a fan. And as much as Fox hated him, he didn't want to make problems for Sasha.

But fuck it. He should have taken her up on her offer to go drinking. He ordered a bottle of vodka to go. After all, he would need a proper can-I-crash-on-your-couch gift. And Ryan was more likely to not give Sasha grief about him showing up if he brought liquor. At least, Fox hoped so. Because as alarming as it was to think about, he had nowhere else to go.

Chapter Three

Sasha rubbed her temples as she tried desperately *not* to throw something.

"Is it so bad that I want to spend more time with my girlfriend?"

Sahsa dragged in a deep breath and prayed for calm. "No, it's not a bad thing, but it would be nice if just once you supported me."

Moving in with her boyfriend was supposed to *help* their relationship. Ryan had been complaining about how much time she spent working at her internship, on her classwork, and at the restaurant.

"I do support you. I just didn't expect you to take me for granted."

She took a deep breath and then another. Take him for granted. Take him for — she was pretty sure, he didn't know what the hell that meant.

"You mean like the several times I've covered for you at work when you've been too hung-over to go in? Or the times you've left your wallet and asked me to go fetch it between class and work and the restaurant just so *you* didn't have to leave work? Or the times I make you dinner and you don't even bother to call and let me know that you're going out with your friends?"

"Shit, are you seriously still mad about that? It happened a couple of times."

She threw up her hands. "It's happened twice this week alone."

This was an old argument. He'd been complaining since the beginning of their relationship that she didn't make enough time for him. So when he floated the idea of moving in together, she'd jumped at the chance, believing it would help the situation. *More like help her need therapy.*

How could he complain they weren't together enough if they were sharing a bed every night, and eating breakfast together? If she sat next to him on the couch most evenings, while she studied for her exams and he watched his reality TV shows? Apparently, Ryan was going for a medal in complaining.

Somehow, being around each other so much had only made Ryan's complaining and jealousy worse, and she had run out of energy and patience to deal with him.

"You're at the news studio more than I am, and I work there *full time*," he yelled at her.

She refrained from pointing out that her internship in story development, with the promise of researching, writing, and filming her own segments, was at a higher level than the editing booth. Ryan helped record the journalists' voiceovers and spliced them together for the video editors to sync up with the final cut of the story. One-upping him would not be helpful.

"There's no way you should be there so much unless there's something else that's keeping you there," Ryan said with growing indignation. "Or maybe I should say...some*one*."

She blinked at him. Then blinked again. "Someone?" she repeated, his implication sinking in and feeding the fury in her chest. "Yes. There's someone keeping me there — me. *I* keep myself there. This internship is everything I've wanted to do with my life. If I stick with it and put as much of myself into it as I can, then I could make my career. If my internship goes well enough, they could hire me full time when I graduate. Do you not appreciate how important that is or why I might be so dedicated to my work?"

"You don't *need* to have your master's degree to work there," Ryan emphasized. "I don't. You could already *be* working there full-time *and* getting paid for it."

"I pay my own way around here, and don't you forget it," Sasha spat back at him.

"Yeah, by waiting tables and working even *more* hours when you could be doing something more worthwhile with your time."

"You mean waiting on you, instead? Is that what you want me around here for? So you don't have to do your own laundry or cook your own meals? Newsflash, Ryan, that wasn't going to happen anyway. I'm not your mother or your babysitter. It's not my job to take care of you."

His face went red, and a twitch above his right eye appeared, making his brow leap spastically.

"Or are you more worried about how it *looks* to have me working there more hours and so much harder than you do? You just don't like the fact that your intern girlfriend is making you look, what...lazy? Unaccomplished?" *Oh, shit. Too late to call that back.*

He glared at her. "I think you're using your pretty face and ass to make me look like the fool who can't see when he's being cheated on," Ryan sneered.

Sasha's palms itched at her sides with the urge, the need, to slap him. Instead she gritted her teeth. That was not going to solve her problem, no matter how satisfying it might be. And in a physical confrontation, she was at a distinct disadvantage.

He'd never touched her like that, but he liked to use his size to crowd and intimidate her sometimes. She might be fit, but he still weighed more than she did and was taller. She wasn't sure if she was quicker, but she didn't want to have to find out.

"Get out," she said with quiet force. "We're done. I want you out of my apartment."

"It's *our* apartment," Ryan reminded her.

"It's my name on the lease. I will call the cops and have you removed if I have to. I am done with your paranoia. I'm done with your whining and with your self-centered…assholery." She swept around the room and picked up his scattered things off the coffee table and the counter and the sofa, throwing them into a pile for him to take. His sweatshirt, an orphaned sock, the empty case to one of his video games. She ushered him toward the door.

"It's McAllister, isn't it?" Ryan sneered, as he made no move to retrieve his things. "He's always staring at your tits. He'd probably promote you to the anchor desk if you gave him a blowjob. Or maybe you have. Maybe he's holding out for more. You know, you really don't have to work as hard as you pretend to. You could easily leverage that face of yours into a career."

"That's all I've ever been to you, isn't it? A

pretty face you could parade around the office and
piss on to show I was yours," Sasha said, fighting
the lump in her throat. "You never actually cared
about me at all. You just wanted to make sure no
one else had me. Well you can fuck off. I'm done
stroking your ego and your limp dick. You can go
back to stroking it for yourself. Lord knows, you're
more than capable."

"Guess you've found someone else's ego to
stroke."

There was a knock on the door.

"You should really stop talking now," Sasha
advised as she went to answer it.

"I'm only just starting, babe," he called back.

She rolled her eyes and took a deep breath
before she pulled the door open. Fox fell into the
apartment, a bottle of vodka rolling across the floor
and into the kitchen.

"Whoa," he said, chuckling as he pushed
himself onto his knees. Sasha reached down and
took hold of his arm to help pull him up. "Sorry
about that," he slurred. "Thought it was the wall I
was leaning against."

"Fox? What are you doing here?" Sasha
asked, confused and embarrassed. Of course, her
best friend would show up here, just as she was
breaking up with Ryan.

"As you can see, I'm drunk." He swayed a little. "Any chance you can let your loser of a bestie crash on your couch? I even brought vodka." Fox dropped back to his knees to search for the wayward bottle.

"I knew it. You've been fucking Fox behind my back, then?" Ryan accused.

Though Fox was preoccupied when Ryan said it, Sasha noticed that he perked up when the words sank in. "What the fuck? Have you lost your mind, dude?" He asked, reaching for the wall and pulling himself to his feet again.

"Fox, leave it," Sasha interjected. "Ryan was just leaving — weren't you, Ryan?"

"The hell I am," he insisted. "I live here, and I'm not about to walk out so you can turn around and fuck your *friend* just to get back at me."

"I've already told you, Ryan, I'm *done* with you. Dumping you, breaking up with you, kicking you to the curb. Pick one." She added, "If you don't want to pack your things now, I can do it and leave them for you to pick up later. In the meantime, just *get out!*"

But Ryan ignored Sasha and focused entirely on Fox, who was blinked rapidly in an attempt to clear his vision.

"I know what you've been up to," Ryan said

slowly to Fox. "Behind my back. I should have known better than to trust you. No way you two were just friends. Sasha's always talking about you. I knew something was up." He sneered. "A fucking Coulter. But you're not one of the famous ones, are you? Is this what you're doing, instead? Going after other guys' girls with your…stick? You know," he said, turning to Sasha, "you'll be needing a sugar daddy to help you pay the rent on this place without me. Maybe you should start your interviews with this one, here."

Fox looked Ryan up and down, then leaned to the side to eye Sasha. "How did you decide on this prick, again?"

"I'm a better choice than a has-been." Ryan grabbed hold of Sasha's arm and gripped tight.

She winced. "Let me go. You're hurting me."

"You're seriously fucking this loser? I have fucking given you every—"

But he didn't get to finish. One second he was getting in her face and gripping her so tightly she was sure he was going to leave bruises, and the next she was free and he was staggering back and howling in pain.

As a goalie, she'd rarely seen Fox engage in the fistfights that were as much a part of hockey as the ice the players skated on, but even falling-down drunk he had better technique and aim than Ryan did.

The first hit made Ryan double over. Ryan swung wildly, just grazing Fox's cheek. Fox's second hit, though--that was the money shot. Fox didn't hit him hard enough to break his nose, but there was enough power behind it to make blood pour over Ryan's lip and into his mouth, staining his teeth and chin. Ryan groaned and clutched his hands to his face. "Son of a bitch! I should sue you for this!"

"No one's suing anyone, Ryan," Sasha said, stepping between the two of them. "Now get the hell out of my apartment. I'll pack your things and leave the boxes outside the door for you to pick up later. Let me get you a cloth for your nose and then you can be on your way. I'm sure Jeff will let you crash with him until you find a place of your own."

Sasha didn't even leave the entryway. Instead, she reached through the pass through window into the kitchen and grabbed a dishrag off the faucet, holding it for Ryan to press to his nose.

Ryan cursed as he continued to swipe and smear the blood coating the lower half of his face.

Fox slunk behind Sasha, out of the way but ready to back her up or force Ryan through the door if she needed him. She didn't. Ryan glared at her as he hovered in the open door.

"Fucking slut," he muttered, as she slammed the door in his face.

Sasha shook her head and leaned against the door.

"Congratulations on getting rid of the douche," Fox said with a smug grin. "Care to toast with that vodka I brought? Hitting that bastard sobered me up a bit, and I'm not ready to be sober yet."

"What the hell are you doing here, Fox?" she asked in a gentle voice that included a hint of annoyance but also gratitude for having helped with Ryan. She took a few steps into the kitchen to retrieve the vodka bottle and set it on the counter.

"I blew it, Sasha. Like I always do," he said as he moved to her couch and dropped onto the overstuffed cushions.

She sighed. "I'm sure you didn't blow it. They were just looking for something different."

"No. I choked. *Again*." He groaned and leaned his head onto the back of the couch, looking up at her ceiling.

She felt bad for him. But she'd never tell him that. He was struggling. He wasn't the only athlete she'd met like this. So many of her father's and grandfather's friends had been through the same thing. Watching him over the years had given her the idea for her story.

Now seeing Fox on the couch with little flecks of Ryan's blood splattered on his shirt, bits of peanut shells stuck to his shoes, and reeking of booze, she wondered again at the long-term psychological impact on professional athletes who'd been trained for nothing else since they were children. Especially those who failed to succeed. She could help people with a story like this—focusing on those who never seemed to reach their promised potential. She slid a glance at her friend. Maybe even help Fox.

She hated seeing him like this. And she knew there was no reasoning with him.

"I'm sorry if I caused a problem with ass-face," Fox said, pushing himself into a more upright position.

"Don't be. I was in the process of breaking up with him when you showed up," she said, crossing the room to drop onto the couch next to him. She put her feet up on the coffee table and turned toward Fox. A wave of alcohol fumes wafted over her, making her eyes water, and she cringed away from him. "Ugh," she groaned, leaning as far away from him as she could. "God, did you spill your beer in the toilet and then roll around in it?"

Fox looked down at his sweatshirt, pinched it between his fingers, and raised the fabric toward his nose to take a sniff. He shrugged and let it drop down again. "It smells like my career, is all."

Sasha laughed wryly. "Come on. Let's get you cleaned up." She stood and reached out a hand to pull him to his feet.

"I'm the only one left, you know," he said. "All my friends on the team—they're all getting their shot." He snorted. "I guess it makes sense I wouldn't get mine. That's my job as a goalie, to block the shots. Wish I was better in the other direction."

"You're not making any sense," Sasha muttered as she tugged him in the direction of the bathroom. "You need to sober up. Then you'll realize that there's no way you're the only one left from your team. I know you can't play hockey with just a goalie. Someone's gotta score the goals on the other team."

"I've scored on myself before," he mumbled. "Does that count?"

She pushed him through the bathroom door. He sat on the toilet fully clothed, and leaned his head against the wall.

"Are you looking to me for an ego boost?" she asked, bending down to pull off his shoes and socks. "If you are, I'm afraid I'm all out." She tossed the shoes back out the bathroom door and into the hallway. "I've been busy stroking Ryan's ego for far too long."

"Is that the only thing his you've been stroking?" Fox teased.

"God, you're as crude as he is." Sasha rolled her eyes and moved to pull Fox's sweatshirt up and over his head. He offered no resistance to her stripping him. It wasn't the first time she'd helped him when he was drunk. Though usually he was sober enough to get into the shower on his own.

"I'm drunk," he stated. "He was a sober prick. Never liked that asshole."

"Yes, you said that before. I don't know how, but I always manage to find them, don't I?" She shook her head at herself as Fox pulled his arms through the sleeves of his T-shirt and tossed it to the floor with his sweatshirt. He wasn't dirty or sweaty. He'd probably showered in the locker room after his tryout.

Her eyes flicked quickly over the lean muscles of his torso, arms, and chest. Jesus, he'd always been hot, but damn. Was that a new tattoo? She studied the small eagle on his shoulder and was careful not to touch it, even if she sort of wanted to.

She swallowed hard as she ran her arm

around his waist. Fox fell somewhere between his brothers in body type. Dax wasn't as bulky as most football players, but he was still the most massive of the Coulter boys. Bryce and Gage were both lean, though Gage had several inches in height on both Bryce and Fox. But Fox had built up noticeable muscle mass while carrying around the weight of his goalie pads. Her eyes drifted down to his thighs, which were snug in his jeans. Skating had definitely given him powerful legs.

Fox caught her looking and grinned. "See something you like?"

She ducked her head. "Be serious, Fox."

"Did you want to help me with my pants, as well, or do you think I can manage those on my own?" He asked with a lazy smirk.

She flushed as he laughed. "I was just making sure you hadn't pissed yourself," she shot back. "Now do you think you can stand without falling over?" She hoped he could because it was one thing to ogle his strong chest, but the full monty might give her a view she didn't bargain on. Her stomach flipped at the thought.

He used the towel bar to help pull himself up, knocking the hand towels off in the process. Looking Sasha square in the eye, he reached down to unbutton his jeans and unzip his fly. With a hard swallow, she kept her eyes on his while he eased his jeans over his hips. He slipped the denim down his legs and stepped out of them, kicking them into the hallway with the rest of his clothes. His boxers stayed on. Holy hell. Her mouth watered.

"What is it that cops have drunk people do again? When they pull them over and make them get out of the car?" His gaze wandered from her to the frosted glass of her shower door.

"I don't have any personal experience with that one, and as far as I'm aware, you don't, either. And I'm certainly not going to let you risk changing that tonight," she said as she turned away to reach the small linen closet next to the shower. She pulled out an oversized towel and handed it to Fox. "You'll sleep on the couch tonight. I think I've got some of your clothes tucked in the back of my closet from the last time you pulled a stunt like this. I'll go see if I can dig them out for you."

"Wait," he said, reaching for her. He missed and crashed against the door of the shower.

"What the hell, Fox?" Sasha muttered, grabbing him by his upper arms to help steady him. "You're supposed to open the door before you try to go through it," she teased when she was certain he hadn't broken anything on either himself or the shower.

"I don't know how this shower works. Hard to do when drunk."

Sasha rolled her eyes and gave him a little push so she could slide past him enough to reach in and turn the water on. "Left is hot, right is cold. Do you think you can remember that?"

He muttered and laughed. "Got it."

She let out a low, breathy laugh. "I'll go find your clothes." Sasha brushed past him and closed the bathroom door behind her, letting out a breath she didn't realize she had been holding.

***

The clothes weren't in the closet where Sasha thought they'd be. Instead, she found the box in question in the spare room that Ryan had promised to help her turn into an office. So far, it only held a beanbag chair, a folding table, cartons filled with some of Ryan's vintage gaming systems, and the box she was searching for.

The box contained all of Fox's things she'd acquired over the years, the miscellaneous articles of clothing and accessories he'd left at the various places she'd lived. She knew he had a similar box at his place for all of the things she'd forgotten to take home with her, too.

Every year or two, they swapped boxes to return each other's stuff and laughed over how long they'd been looking for the contents. As she looked at the box tucked away in the corner next to the gaming systems Ryan said he was going to sell on eBay, she realized just how much she'd had to adjust to accommodate Ryan and his petty jealousies.

She should have known better than to start dating him in the first place. She was already swamped with her schoolwork and working at the restaurant. She knew she didn't have the time to devote to a relationship. But he had been so encouraging in the beginning, hadn't he? It was difficult to remember just how things had been in those early days. He was the one with the internship at the station, getting ready to graduate in just a few months.

He'd had a few credits left to take, and was due to graduate in the winter. He had seemed impressed by the fact that she was applying for the same internship the following spring semester. When the station offered him a job, it had just been easier to let things progress since they'd be able to see one another whenever she was on site for her internship.

Sasha laughed humorlessly. That was her pattern, then. She got involved with him because he was going to be around anyway. He was a constant, and she didn't have to think. And shit, he'd paid a lot of attention to her. She'd moved in with him so they'd have more time together because just working together wasn't enough for Ryan. Her focus had always been on the work, and his focus had always been on her and having as much of her as she would let him take. And still, it wasn't enough for him.

As she hefted the box of Fox's belongings into her arms and carried it down the hall to their bedroom—*her* bedroom—to put back in her closet, she glanced at Ryan's things scattered about and wondered if she would feel anything with him gone. They'd been together for almost a year. There had been moments of fun, but lately it was like her relationship was the distraction and her work was where she was enjoying herself. Wasn't it supposed to be the other way around? What she felt was relief, pure and simple.

She should feel bad about Fox punching Ryan. That would be the adult thing to do. But she found it oddly amusing. And butterflies fluttered low in her belly when she thought about the look on Fox's face when he'd hit him. Ryan had been hurting her, and there was no way Fox would ever let that happen.

She knocked on the bathroom door with a set

of clothes for Fox tucked under her arm. "Fox?" she called. "I'm going to leave your clean clothes on the floor just outside the door. Okay?"

There was no response from inside.

"Fox?" she called again. "Just say, 'okay' and I'll leave you alone. I need you to let me know you're all right."

There was still no answer.

Given how drunk he was, she didn't want to take any chances on him doing damage to himself or her bathroom. She was counting on that security deposit.

The doorknob turned—he hadn't locked it when she left. When she saw that he was in the shower with his boxers on, she was both relieved and amused. She stepped into the bathroom and set his clothes on the counter next to the sink.

He was sitting on the floor of the shower with his back to the water. She didn't think he was crying, but he was hanging his head.

"Can you stand up?" she asked, banging her hand lightly on the frosted glass.

His head jerked up, and he looked completely broken. He looked terrible, having slipped from his jolly drunken state into a self-pitying condition that he generally had a difficult time escaping without help.

"Christ," she said under her breath. Impulsively, she pulled off her own shirt and pants. She opened the door to the shower and climbed in, turning the water temperature up a bit higher. She gave herself a moment to get used to the water and let it soak her hair and underwear before she crouched carefully beside Fox and reached out to touch him.

"Come on," she said gently. "Let's get you cleaned up. Can you turn around a bit? Come on, up you go." Sasha tried to hide the concern in her voice.

She tried not to pay any attention to the expanse of muscle in front of her, trying to ignore the colorful tattoos that wound around Fox's arms and chest, the light fuzz that dusted his pecs, and the trail of dark hair from his belly button to— she glanced down.

Oh, holy hell.

The cotton fabric of his boxer briefs clung to him. And there was no mistaking the outline of his—. She swallowed hard. This was not why she was here. She was here to help him.

Once she had him on his feet, she turned around and reached for the shower gel and sponge. Gently, she lathered him up from shoulder to shoulder and down his pecs to the expanse of his abs.

Jesus, that really is a damn washboard.

When most of the blood was gone, she turned him again and lifted the showerhead to help rinse him off. She watched as the soap trails ran off of his perfect body, licking her lips nervously.

No. You are not here to ogle him. You are here to get him clean, to sober him up.

She added more gel to the sponge and moved to his face, gently wiping away the blood cresting his nose and upper lip.

"You know you didn't have to do that," she said softly.

Fox's lips turned up in a weak, lopsided smile. "Yes, I did. He put his hands on you. I had to make sure he remembered to never do that again."

"I don't like you fighting over me," Sasha said.

He shook his head, "One-time deal, I promise. It's just, when I saw his hand on you, I wasn't exactly thinking straight."

"Yeah, well, I hate to see you hurt."

He grinned. "You should see the other guy."

Sasha shook her head. "Let me rephrase that. I hate to see you hurting anyone on my behalf. You and I both know I can take care of myself."

His gaze locked on her lips for a moment. "I know that. Still, I'm never going to be okay with him putting his hands on you like that. There has to be some benefit from having a friend as big as me. That way, you get to walk softly and carry a big stick."

Oh, shit. He said stick.

This made her mind immediately drift to the length of his erection pressing into her hip. It was as if he knew she was thinking about it. Resolutely, she kept her gaze on his eyes. She saw the flicker of mischievousness in them. She also saw something else. Was it interest? No, this was Fox. He was a flirt. He had swaths of women lined up for him. His last name played a big part in that because he had money, but the main reason women lined up for Fox Coulter was his damn face. The guy could easily be a movie star with his full lips, high cheekbones, and that straight, regal nose. His deep-set eyes burned a bright blue every time he gazed at her.

I'm going to combust.

Then there was his body. He had a ridiculous build, the kind you had to work hard for, but not overly done. He was tall and muscular, but lean at the same time.

"Just go ahead and ignore that big stick. I've had a lot to drink, and as far as he's concerned, you're a warm, available female. Don't mind him."

She tried to deflect. "What is this stick you speak of?"

The thick length of him twitched again, almost causing her to moan. When was the last time she had a good, old-fashioned, toe-curling orgasm?

Hell, when was the last time I even had the opportunity?

Ryan didn't like kissing. He thought it was weird, so for over a year no one had even kissed her properly. The kind of kisses that made the panties wet, the hair wild, and the belly buzz and flip around. Man, she missed those kinds of kisses.

Fox licked his bottom lip. As he leaned in closer, Sasha held her ground and kept her gaze locked on his.

"Sash—" the way he said her name was more of a question. As if he were trying to determine what was happening. Trying to decide if he should give in to their tension. Trying to figure out what the hell they were doing.

Sasha took a deliberate step back. She reminded herself that she had no desire to be yet another notch on Fox Coulter's bedpost. The Coulter boys were notorious, from Bryce all the way down to Gage. Fox was no different from his brothers. His exploits were legendary. He'd told Sasha about most of them himself.

Do you really want to be one of those girls, one of those groupies?

Hell, yes! Her libido screamed even as her mind tried to talk her out of it. Regardless, she still had no desire to be another notch.

Sasha purposefully positioned the showerhead between them, rinsing him off. By gently cupping some water, she began washing away the soap that was on his face. He looked normal with all the blood washed away, back to her Fox. The spell had been broken, and the two best friends hadn't crossed any lines they couldn't come back from. Everything was just about back to normal.

Thank God.

"Come on, Fox," she said, wringing out the cloth and letting the water soak it again. "There's more to this. You've been through this before and you never got this bad. And it's more than just some of your friends getting the call and not you. Spill." She kept washing him, telling herself it was for his benefit. *Liar.*

The noise he made was somewhere between a sigh and a moan. "I'm a Coulter," he stated flatly.

"I've noticed."

"Coulters don't fail. We just...don't. Except me. I fail. I'm a failure." He said with quiet conviction.

Sasha dropped the washcloth to floor and reached over to pull him toward her, resting his wet head against her shoulder, enveloping his big body in her own. "You are not a failure, and your family isn't perfect. Look at your grandfather. He didn't medal in the Olympics."

"No, he just helped Gram defect and then won two Super Bowls."

"And your dad...he was better at basketball than baseball," she said, ignoring his counter-arguments.

"He still made the pros for both."

"Bryce choked his first time in the semi—"

"He didn't choke, he blew out his knee."

"I'm trying to make you feel better," she reminded him with a hard squeeze of his shoulder.

"Yeah, well you suck at it. No wonder the prick is looking for someone else to stroke his *ego*," Fox said. "Ego-stroking takes a firm grip, and finesse, and knowing just when to tease."

Sasha barked a laugh even as she flushed. Because the fact that he made the joke meant she was succeeding in cheering him up. Also, because listening to him say it while they were both in their sopping wet underwear in her shower struck her as particularly funny.

"Your tits are huge," he said, as he nuzzled into her cleavage. "Seriously, they're like big soft pillows. Keep laughing like that. It's really comfy."

She was laughing even harder when she gave his head a small shove off her chest. Because while he was making her laugh, he was also making her warm and tingly deep inside. She reached past him to turn off the water, letting it go cold for a moment before turning it off completely. She could still feel the warmth of his cheek pressed into her flesh, his shoulder and arm against her belly as she'd held him.

After a long moment, she stood, stepped out, and grabbed the towel she'd set out for him, wrapping it around herself and going to the linen closet to fetch another one for him. "I guess I have a few things to figure out now. I'm not sorry Ryan's moving out. Don't get me wrong."

"But you're gonna miss the extra paycheck?" Fox finished for her, using his hands to brush as much of the water from his body as he could.

He didn't appear to notice her holding the towel out for him as he slid his fingers through his hair to squeeze out more water. Sasha cleared her throat and looked away from the sight of his waterlogged boxers clinging to, uh …man parts. It was…distracting.

"Oh, thanks," he muttered, taking the towel and covering himself. "If you want, I can stay here and pay you rent. Then we'd be roomies and we wouldn't need to spend half our nights on the phone dissecting Mr. Robot."

Sasha laughed. "You're not serious."

"Why not?" Fox asked as he leaned against the doorframe with his hand holding the towel together at his waist. Shit, did he even know what he looked like? All lean muscle, and tattoos. *Wet and…sexy.* Wait, what? This was Fox. He was her friend.

Sasha's grip on her own towel tightened. "Because I do not need my apartment overrun by hockey groupies. I'll…figure something out."

He rolled his eyes. "It wouldn't be that bad. Besides, I do understand what discretion means. And obviously the whole 'sugar daddy' thing doucheface said was complete bullshit. I don't mind the couch for tonight or whatever. I can't keep crashing on my other friends' couches — not…*now*…"

She had opened her mouth to object, but Sasha realized why he didn't want to crash with those friends anymore before she actually said anything. He could take their hospitality when they were teammates, but now it would be tainted with pity rather than camaraderie.

"And I wouldn't mind a real bed now and then that didn't require awkward meals with my parents. With Gage at college, I'm the only one left there. I can't take that much attention," he explained, his gaze pleading.

Sasha wanted to say yes. He was going through a rough patch right now, and she wanted to help. And she couldn't deny how useful it would be to have his help paying the bills. But she was afraid. They were already too close. And if he was under her roof, she worried she'd slip-up and he'd see that hidden kernel of hope that he'd one day look at her as more than just his friend. Hope was such a stupid thing.

What's more, with both of them standing in her bathroom in nothing more than wet underwear and bath towels, she was too aware of that line in their friendship that she knew was better left uncrossed. Jokes that were fine when she had a boyfriend or when he had a girlfriend were a gray area now. But with the forced intimacy of living together…there might be two bedrooms, but there was still only *one* bathroom. She wasn't sure what that might do to their friendship, and she didn't think she was ready to find out.

Not to mention, Fox was hell on women. She knew him well. There would be half-naked women around here in no time. She was so close to getting her degree, and if the internship continued on as well as it was going, she might even have a job when she was done.

"I don't think that would be a good idea," she said cautiously. "It's just... I need to...stay focused on things right now. That was my big mistake with getting involved with Ryan. He was too much of a distraction." She headed out of the bathroom and he followed on her heels.

"What makes you think I'd be a distraction?" Fox asked as he held up a hand to keep her from laughing. He gestured to his chest. "You know what? Don't bother answering that. You're right. I'm hot. But just so you know, it's an open offer. If you have a hard time at all and change your mind..." He winked.

"Get your clothes on," she scolded him, even as she chuckled.

"Consider my night on the couch tonight as an audition," he called over his shoulder as she departed for her bedroom. "I won't even sleep naked... Unless, you want me to. You know what? I suggest having naked roommate night. C'mon. It'll be fun."

"You are incorrigible," she called out.

"I don't even know what that means."

After Sasha closed her bedroom door, she leaned back against it, willing her heart to stop pounding and trying to convince herself the rush of heat in her lower belly was nothing more than a biological response.

No, having him living with her would definitely be more of a distraction than she could handle at the moment. Their friendship was one of the few things in her life that she could count on. While her jobs and school were going well for her, they weren't exactly stress-free. Hanging out with Fox was a great way for her to relax, and she desperately needed that. No reason to go and make something complicated that didn't need to be.

Chapter Four

It wasn't like Fox was really sneaking into his own house, he was merely trying to avoid seeing anyone. Particularly his grandfather. But sure enough, as he rounded the corner into the study, Gramps was the first one he saw. He stopped abruptly, hoping the old man hadn't seen him, but it was too late for that.

"Fox?"

He sighed. "Hey, Gramps."

"Well, fancy seeing you here. You couldn't sleep in your bed last night?"

Fox let that one slide. The old man could fish as much as he wanted.

"I had some things to take care of." He pondered to himself, *Yeah, like having a fitful night of dreams of my best friend. Those soft lips. And God, her breasts.*

The memory alone of his face pressed into her tits, water raining down on them, was enough to give him wet dreams for a month. He tried to remind himself that she was Sasha, his best friend. He needed to get her tits off his mind. Normally, he was able to forget that Sasha was a girl. They were best friends and confidants as teenagers, even as children. Although, at one point he was convinced that she had cooties, but after that phase they became thick as thieves.

"Well, Gramps, I'd love to chat, but I have some things—"

"Just wait a second, Fox. How did it go yesterday?"

Yesterday was the last thing he wanted to talk about. "You know how these things go, Gramps. I wasn't who they were looking for this time."

His grandfather shook his head, "They don't seem to understand that you're a Coulter. Don't name and legacy mean anything? They are fools. Like I've been telling you for years, you need to change sports. You're big enough...play football. We can get you a private coach to work with you. I have pull, and believe I could get you some tryouts."

Fox took a deep breath, trying to remain calm. "Gramps, I don't want to change sports. I love hockey, it's been my whole life. Hockey to me, is like football to you."

Gramps sat back in his chair. "Well, listen to me. From the sounds of it, you won't make the cut again. How long do you think you have before they stop calling you up in the first place?"

That was the last thing he needed to hear. "Gramps, I'm going to head to my room."

"Don't sulk. That's conduct unbecoming a Coulter. If you'll let me help you, I can have a coach here tomorrow."

"Shit—dammit, Gramps! Just give it a rest. You would think you'd have learned your lesson by now after Bryce and Dax. But you still can't help it. You just push, push, push your agenda." Fox took a deep breath. "This is why I stayed with Sasha last night. Just so I could avoid this conversation."

Immediately, Fox wished he could take back those words. They would just give his grandfather another issue to press. It would make the old man happy to see him and Sasha together. After all, Gramps and Sasha's grandfather had played ball together.

Gramps lit up. "I always did like that girl. You'd be doing well if you'd snag her up before someone else does. She's pretty enough to be any pro athlete's wife. With her connections, she won't stay off the market for long."

Why did I bother coming home again?

Fox shook his head. "Please, I'm begging you. Just stop."

"I don't know why the lot of you walk around here being as ungrateful as you are. I am the patriarch of the family. The glue that holds us together. It's my name that you bear. You don't want to listen to me about your career or your prospects, fine. You don't want to be with Sasha, fine. It's probably better anyway, given how her father blew his entire fortune. That girl needs a meal ticket. And we don't want another golden-haired goddess with her claws sunk into this family."

"Gramps, that's enough."

"Fox is right, Dad. Give it a rest."

Fox turned to find his father in the doorway. His color was better than usual. But still, he looked tired. A shadow wound its way around Fox's spine, as the warmth settled into his body. His father looked improved, but was he actually better? How long would he remain better, if he kept pushing at the pace he was?

"Hi, Dad."

"Hi, Fox. We heard from Echo. Sorry about the trials."

More pity. Just what I needed.

Fox shrugged. "I'll get it next time. I'll see you later. I'm going to grab some stuff from my room before heading to practice."

Fox ran out of the room as fast as his legs could carry him. He didn't run to escape his grandfather, or even the specter of his father's illness. He ran from the pity, as it was the last thing he wanted to deal with.

I don't need their pity. Dammit, I'm a Coulter, not a washout. I can't be.

***

"What aspects do you want me to change?" Sasha took out paper and pen, ready to take as many notes as necessary as she sat in Ida's office.

Ida shook her head. "Not many, actually. Just one major thing. We want you to focus on a central character, sort of like a case study. Yes, you're talking about the effect that this amount of pressure can have on these young athletes well into adulthood. I just don't think we can properly illuminate that without actually using someone specific as an example."

Sasha waited for Ida to mention a certain local high school kid, for whom everyone had big plans. He made it to college, but busted his knee during his first game. His injury caused him to lose his scholarship, so he pretty much came back home to San Diego and started at a community college. He was trying to get his life back on track.

Sasha pointed to the young man's name on the list. "You mean him?"

"No, closer to home than that. Fox Coulter. You know him, right? The word is he's a very good friend of yours. Other rumors are centered around the fact that he has been trying to make it to the major league NHL for years. Coming from a family like the Coulters? That's huge! You should use that."

Sasha sat up straighter. "You want me to do the story about Fox?" She repeated what Ida had said in the vain hope that she had heard incorrectly. There was no way that her boss, her mentor, was asking her to throw her best friend under the bus for a story.

"Exactly." Ida shrugged. "Well, in a manner of speaking. But if you use the template as a starting point, we can go from there. Expand on what you're hypothesizing. I think it'd be great, and seeing as you two are friends, he'd be a perfect subject to focus on because you know him so well."

"Ida, I don't think I can do that. He's my friend," Sasha protested. "There are things that he's told me in confidence. Things he would never tell anyone else."

"Exactly! You can get to the heart of the matter, your friend, and also become a journalist. We're not naming names. Why would I call him out? You can see what his attempts are doing to his psyche. Your relationship will inform your questions when you go talk to experts and psychologists."

"I'm not doing the story on Fox. Do you have any idea how hurt he would be?"

"I understand." Ida said. "And I'm not asking you to do a story on Fox Coulter. I'm asking you to do the story you pitched, just with Fox Coulter in mind. He makes a great case study. He's young and has had every advantage known to man, but still can't make it. So if someone like him can't make it with an athletic gene pool like his, then what's it really like for normal people?"

Sasha tried to sort it all out in her head. *Use Fox to inform my story? No. I can't do that.*

"I'm pretty sure he wouldn't be down for it."

"Sasha, you're a smart kid," Ida replied. "And you look beautiful on camera. I think with a story like this you can make your mark. Like I said, I'm not asking you to give up the source, and I'm not asking you to do a story about Fox. I think you can talk to him and use some of what he tells you as a way to map out your story. Take a little time to think about it and let me know."

Sasha watched her boss walk away. What was she supposed to do? The tiny voice in her head spoke again. *Well, it's not about him. It's about pressure from people like his grandfather and the rest of his family and what that does to him.*

Sasha got an idea. There might be a way to do this story without using Fox at all. She had thought of another athlete to use as her focus, and that might work. Ida didn't need to know, and that way she didn't have to hurt Fox. The only drawback was that Fox would eventually see the story.

Would he recognize some of himself? Not if I don't use him as a template. She could interview some of his brothers. Bryce, Dax — hell, even Echo. *Yeah, that could work.* They'd all seen their share of adversity.

Sasha was friends with all of them. They all grew up together, but Fox was always her *best* friend. This might just work, and she could leave Fox out of her story.

Once her brain worked out a way around the Fox issue, the excitement set in. They really liked her proposal. She could do amazing things. She could help people. Her goal was within reach.

Chapter Five

For Sasha, the next week and a half passed in a whirlwind of school, internship, school, work, internship, and work again. The restaurant was a high-end place, so the tips were generally pretty good. But parties also tended to take their time making the turnover was slow which unfortunately, balanced things out in the end.

She'd probably have been able to make more if she worked as a bartender, but that would require taking a class and she was stretched thin as it was. She hadn't found a new roommate yet, and desperation was becoming a thing with rent coming due in another week along with the electricity and water bills.

"Hey, Freddie, how's your apartment hunt going?" she asked the bartender, Frederica, while waiting for her to mix the drinks she needed for table seven. "I've got an extra room that's up for grabs."

Freddie's smile was strained as she concentrated on the shaker in her hands, the noise of the ice too loud for her to answer right away. "Sorry, Sash," Freddie said as she poured out the drink and added its garnish. "I just finished unpacking at my new place. It's smaller than a closet, but the view over the water is worth it. Not to mention the rent is manageable with me all by my lonesome."

Damn, she'd taken too long to ask. "Yeah, I figured, but it was worth a shot," Sasha said as she carefully placed the drinks on the serving tray.

"You haven't gotten back together with Ryan, then?"

"Nope. There will be no mending of anything with Ryan," she said. "I'm through making excuses for his general douchery, and I'm done wasting my time and energy on carrying his ego around for him. He picked up the last of his things while I was in class yesterday morning and then I had the locks changed. That's the last I have to see of him...except when I'm at the station."

"God, working with your ex like that... It must suck," Freddie said as she set the shaker in the bin of dirty dishes and glasses waiting for one of the busboys to take it to the kitchen. A clean bin sat on her other side, waiting for her to restock the bar.

"It is surprising how little time we actually spent together, considering we work at the same place. But then that was one of the things he'd been complaining about, so..."

"Well, good luck on your roommate search.

If I hear anyone asking around I'll let you know."

"Thanks, Freddie." Sasha scurried off to deliver the drinks to her table.

She spotted her graduate advisor over at the far end of the bar. Dr. Gibbons caught her eye and indicated she wished to speak with Sasha. So at the first chance she got, she sidled up to the older woman's seat, positioning herself so she could keep an eye on the tables in her section.

"Sasha," Dr. Gibbons greeted her warmly. "I wasn't expecting to see you here tonight."

"I picked up an extra shift when one of the other servers called in sick," she explained. She'd put in a request with her manager to get called first whenever something like that happened so she could make as much extra money as possible. It was making things difficult at her internship, but hopefully she would find a roommate and she could go back to the schedule she kept before Ryan moved out.

"Well, it must be fate, because I just have to tell you that I finished going over your proposal, and I love it. The sports angle is a great one for exploring something that's relevant across the board. It's a subject that ties in beautifully to our culture at large. Always pushing to succeed, to win, to get to the top, secure the American Dream and all that, but do we push too hard? Should we be preparing people for failure? Or does acknowledging the fact that we could fail hinder us? So many wonderful questions and I can't wait to see what you discover."

"So I'm good to go ahead and get started on it?"

"Absolutely," Dr. Gibbons assured her after taking a sip of her wine. "You've really taken the initiative on this. I don't usually get proposals until the week of the deadline, and then I have to ride students to meet the later deadlines. You're definitely ahead of the game, making my life easier, and yours, too, if you want to know."

At that moment, Fox walked into the restaurant with several of his friends, and Sasha doubted the wisdom of Dr. Gibbons' words as guilt tied her stomach into knots. She shook herself out of it. Just because Ida wanted her to use Fox, it didn't mean she was going to. This was fine. Everything would work out.

"Thanks, Dr. Gibbons," Sasha said as she moved away from her advisor. "I've gotta get back to work."

Sarah, one of the other waitresses, led Fox and his friends into one of the three rooms the restaurant set aside for private parties. She and

Sarah shared that section. Which meant they'd be sharing the serving duties and splitting the tips when it was over. Sasha wasn't sure whether it was good thing or a bad thing. She and Fox hadn't seen each other since the night he stayed on her couch. She got the distinct impression he was embarrassed. And God knew she was embarrassed about the way she'd been salivating over him. It was an aberration. They'd get back to normal eventually. She hoped.

***

Fox had put it off as long as he could, but he knew his friends would talk if he didn't do something to help them celebrate. He couldn't sulk forever, right? Besides, he was the partier. The partner. The fun one. He could pretend for them. He'd planned it all so he could also shuffle some cash Sasha's way.

It wasn't as though she would take money from him as a loan, and she hadn't said anything more about his offer to move in with her. Though given the massive hard-on he'd woken up with the morning after he'd stayed over, that was probably for the best. She'd *just* broken up with her boyfriend. And if he went there with her, that would ruin everything.

He ordered the first bottle of champagne, nodding a greeting to Sasha when she came into the room with place settings. She gave him a wry smile in return. Once the initial round of toasts was over, things went downhill quick. Dougie and Gerry had split a bottle of rum, while Martin was doing a number on a bottle of whiskey. Fox was relieved he'd sprung for the private room, afraid the restaurant's management might not let him and his friends come back again if they had been seated in the general area, considering the drunken racket.

"Don't worry, buddy," Gerry slurred as he devoured a plate of bruschetta topped with mango and avocado salsa. "Your turn'll come. The guy we've got now…" he snapped his fingers a few times "…Brodie…Brewdie…Brewer." He blinked but couldn't force his tongue to pronounce the name correctly.

"I know who you mean," Fox muttered. Now he was sure this had been a bad idea.

"Right. Anyhoo. He's old, right? So he'll be retiring before you know it. So they'll be putting this new guy, Henri, into the main spot, and they'll need *you* then," Gerry explained the matter like it was a simple equation. "You just gotta sit tight and hang in there."

Fox forced a smile and nodded to feign his reassured state. It was enough for Gerry, drunk as he was, to believe he'd genuinely helped. Gerry took another swig of rum, half of which missed his mouth and trailed down the side of his neck and into the collar of his shirt.

Sasha walked through to check on them, and Fox caught her rolling her eyes at the mess his friends had made. Before she headed out, she caught his eye and he did his best to shrug an apology, but she didn't seem to be in a joking mood. He'd had a glass of champagne during the toasting, but had switched to water after that. He'd already had more than enough to drink after the tryouts.

"D'you know her?" Martin asked after Sasha had left the room.

"Sasha? Yeah. I've known her pretty much my whole life. Our grandfathers played football together," Fox explained. His gaze trailed after Sasha, and for some reason, he couldn't drag it away.

"D'you think you could put in a good word for me?" Martin asked.

Fox clenched his jaw. He wanted to tell Martin to fuck off and leave her alone. *She's mine.* What the hell was wrong with him? He had no idea *where* that shit came from. He couldn't keep thinking about her stroking…or even better, licking, his…ego. "You want to ask her out, that's on you. I'm not getting involved," Fox said carefully. "I will tell you that she just broke up with her boyfriend, and she's not really looking for something right now."

"Great. That means she's down to ride."

Fox narrowed his gaze when he realized his little bit of information had only made Martin *more* interested in Sasha.

"And that's cool, 'cause I'm not looking for more than a ride," Martin continued. "You know how it is, Coulter. Hit it and quit it. And that girl, she looks fun. All that sexy dark hair. Her tits on display. That tight ass?" Martin bit his knuckle, then laughed and nudged Dougie, who chortled and snorted as he raised another shot's worth of rum to his lips.

"Yeah that's…not what I meant at all," Fox muttered between clenched teeth. Martin rose from the table and threw back a bit more whiskey before marching off in the direction Sasha had just gone. He wasn't gone long.

"Bitch told me to fuck off," Martin complained, sitting down again. "You've got some shitty friends there, Fox."

"Don't I know it," he said, heading to find Sasha so he could apologize for Martin's undoubtedly inappropriate behavior.

He spotted her leaning against the bar with

her tray on the bar top. She had her arms crossed and was leaning her head against her forearms. She looked exhausted, and he had a moment of panic where he thought she might be crying.

When the bartender came over with the drinks she was waiting for, she slipped a little shot of something to Sasha, who thanked her friend and downed it in a single gulp.

"Fortifying yourself to come back and glare at me some more?" he asked as he sidled up to her. She jumped.

"Fox... What the hell are you doing out here? Shouldn't you be in the room, supervising those apes you call friends?" She turned away from him to adjust the drinks on the tray and wipe a hair out of her eyes. No, it wasn't a stray hair. It was a tear.

"He's a dead man," Fox muttered under his breath.

"Please. Your friend is nothing I can't handle," Sasha assured him, but there was a thickness in her voice that he picked up on immediately. "He... I've dealt with way worse customers. He wasn't even the grabbiest. And he's not the first I've had to turn down as far as hitting on me goes."

"You shouldn't have to deal with it at all," Fox groaned. "You're just doing your job, and he's had *way* too much to drink—which is entirely *my* fault—and now… I'll… I'll—"

"You'll do nothing because I'm fine. I'll get over it. It's just been a long day already, and things are riding much closer to the surface than I usually keep them," she confessed. "He…he didn't know what he was saying—or doing—and… He called me a sweet piece of ass, and said I should…I should quit working *in* the restaurant, because I'd make a killing working *behind* the restaurant." There was shame in her voice, as she whispered the last part to Fox.

Fox closed his eyes and sucked in a deep breath. "Do you want me to hold him so you can hit him? 'Cause I'll do that. Trust me, it can really help to just hit something once in a while."

Sasha laughed. "Thanks for the offer. I'll be sure to keep it in mind. It could've been worse. He could have tried putting his hand *up* my skirt instead of just on my ass, but I don't think he had the coordination for that tonight."

"Forget me holding him. I'll tie him to a tree and we can *both* hit him."

Sasha sighed. "I'm just tired. It's exhausting. All I am is a face, an ass, and a pair of boobs. I mean…my father always told me to capitalize on my looks while I could—to find some rich guy to marry, and then pop out a few kids for him, and I'd never have to worry about money or anything like that again. It was humiliating *then* and *now*... *Now* it's just..." She was dangerously close to tears.

Fox wanted to pull her into a hug, but he also knew that was probably the *worst* thing to do to Sasha at a moment like that. She never cried. Except when she was ready to blow.

"You'd think I'd be used to all of the ways that men know how to insult a girl — that I'd be able to...distance myself from it better. But...every once in a while...something just...makes it through. What if...what if I really *am* nothing more than just a pretty face and a piece of ass? I want to work on camera. If I get that chance, is it because of my talent and the work I put into researching and writing my stories, or would it just be because I look good on-screen and can read words off a monitor without it *looking* like I'm reading directly off the monitor?"

Fox laughed. She was spinning out.

"It's not funny," Sasha cried. But there was a little twitch to her mouth that suggested she had run out of steam.

"Sure it is. After all this time, if you don't know just how smart you are, then you're dumb. You've been running circles around me academically since...since you learned the alphabet before I did when we were three."

She laughed some more. "Woohoo, I'm smarter than you. I am a woman after all." She teased, a small smile tugging at her lips.

"Ouch. I will have you know that I am brilliant, if only because I can see just how brilliant *you* are. Wasn't there some famous dead old guy who said something about the wise man knowing that he doesn't know everything?"

"You're paraphrasing, but yeah, Socrates said something along those lines."

"Look, I'm sorry about Martin. He's an asshole."

"I noticed."

"And if he has a shred of decency, he'll be too ashamed of himself in the morning to ever even consider speaking to you again. So let me apologize on his behalf. And I'm going to make sure you get home all right tonight. Okay?" He would be dealing with Martin, but he wouldn't tell her that.

Sasha nodded to someone behind Fox, and lifted her tray of drinks. "You don't have to do that."

"No, I do. We look after each other, remember?"

"I guess we do."

Fox watched her paste a smile on her face as

she chatted with her customers. He wasn't sure how she managed to do it, but she deserved so much better than this crappy waitressing job to make ends meet. And he was going to help her. He just needed to figure out how.

When he returned to the party room, he motioned over to Martin and took his bottle. "You're done with this," he explained. Then he moved over to Dougie and Gerry and took their nearly-empty bottle of rum.

"What'd that bitch say? I just asked her out," Martin protested.

The tether on Fox's self-control snapped, and he crowded his friend. "That 'bitch' is my fucking friend, so you need to shut your fucking trap or I'll do it for you."

Martin wasn't so drunk that his brain didn't recognize the danger. He glowered at Fox, but he backed down. Fox's demonstration had quieted Dougie and Gerry as well, turning the loud and raucous celebration into a silent and awkward mess.

Sasha and Sarah came in to see if there was anything more they needed. But when all four of them announced they were finished, Fox asked for the check. Sasha caught Fox's eye and raised an inquisitive brow, but he just turned his attention to Martin to be sure he didn't try to pull anything. Fox had been pissed he hadn't made the team, but now he wondered if he wasn't lucky.

Once he paid the check, he muttered, "I already called you guys an Uber. You can go ahead without me. I have a few things I need to take care of, but I'll talk to you sometime soon." Yeah, like never. Fox suddenly realized that without the team, they didn't have much in common.

***

When she finished her shift, Sasha found Fox waiting for her down in the restaurant's parking lot.

"What're you still doing here? You guys left three hours ago."

"I told you I'd make sure you got home all right," he reminded her. "The others left, but I hung out at the sports bar next door for a while. They had the preseason football games on, so I watched Dax's team. He and the other starters were pulled after the first quarter."

Sasha shook her head. "That's fine, whatever. The tip you left for Sarah and me, it was too much for a party of four, even if you *were* in a private room."

Fox shifted awkwardly. "Oh…well, I know that you're…you know — with the whole Ryan thing." He shrugged. "Besides, look at it as hazard pay for dealing with Martin."

"I have my own car here," Sasha pointed out. "I don't really need a ride."

He grinned. "Good, because I don't have my car with me. I was supposed to be designated driver when we took Dougie's car, but after what happened with Martin, I called them an Uber and told them to come back and get Dougie's car in the morning."

"So *you* need a ride," Sasha laughed and shook her head.

"I could Uber. I just wanted to get you home."

"No," she said, still laughing. "I'll drive you home."

"Please don't," Fox begged as he climbed into the passenger seat of Sasha's four-door sedan. "My parents will ask how tonight went with the guys, and I don't want to get into it."

"Right."

"Or they'll want to talk about Dax's game tonight. Which I know they don't *mean* to make it sound like a dig, but that's what it will feel like anyway."

"You want to crash on my couch again?" she asked.

"I wouldn't have to crash if you let me move in."

"I *should* start charging you rent," she joked.

"Wasn't that what I offered, like, two weeks ago? Are you reconsidering? I promise it doesn't have to be long term." He sat up straighter, more enthusiastic. "It can just be until you find someone else—a month or two. As soon as you get so much as a nibble, I can grab my stuff and get out."

Sasha sighed. He really was very cute. She hadn't meant to reopen that can of worms, but she was too tired. She was still confused about how she felt about the prospect. *You're not confused. You know how you feel about it. Hot.*

They got along well, but would that change when they had to share things like a bathroom and a kitchen? They had crashed with each other plenty over the years, but it was always a situation where one of them was the host and the other the guest. If they lived together and things were truly shared... *Or you saw him naked.*

The thing was, she knew him. And Fox was a flirt. *And you've lusted after him for years.* But he didn't know that. And she wanted to keep it that way. But she also needed the help. Matter of fact, she was desperate.

"Fine. Three months at the most. And only

because I really need the money right now. Once I have something else figured out, then you go. Back to your parent's or into a place of your own, I don't care. And I'll be coming up with a roommate list of rules and guidelines, got it? First on the list—no walking around naked."

"Until you beg." He winked. "Sure, sure. You're the boss," Fox said, holding his hands up in a gesture of surrender, but when he turned to look out the window he was grinning. Sasha tried and failed to tamp down the twitching impulse to smile as well.

Chapter Six

Sasha had a day off two days later to help officially move in Fox and his stuff. There wasn't much extra space in the apartment, but while he'd been at his parents' house throwing what he considered the essentials into duffel bags and plastic bins, she'd made a run to the store and had picked up a few things he'd probably need. He'd never been on his own before. The dude knew nothing about having his own place.

"What…is…that?" he pointed after depositing some of his stuff in the hallway just outside his new room.

"Just a few essentials," Sasha said with a smile. "Mirror, some organizational stuff for your closet…" She flicked the switch to an aqua-colored lava lamp, and the thick orbs began to separate out and circle each other. "Mood lighting," she teased. "Okay, that one is actually from my parents' house. I don't want you to feel like living here is going to…cramp your style or…hinder your, uh, social life with the ladies." She waggled her eyebrows while shuffling around and humming "*I can't get no, satisfaction*".

Fox laughed and shook his head. "That

would imply that I have a life beyond hockey. And as you know better than anyone else, I don't."

"As if I've never seen the groupies. But anyway, I figured you may or may not eventually have, uh, company." Sasha flicked the lava lamp back off. She had also purchased a small plastic set of drawers that she had tucked into a corner of the room. "For your clothes," she explained, when she saw his confusion. "When you said you had ordered a bed, you never said anything about a dresser."

"How much did you spend on this stuff? I thought the whole point of my moving in here with you was so that you could save a bit of money," he reminded her.

"I saved the receipts so you could reimburse me," she grinned. "Since I have the bigger bedroom, including a massive closet, I think you should have the storage closet across the hall for your stuff. I think part of it is meant to be for coats, but I've got that hanging rack thing on the back of the door." Fox looked around his new room as she moved out into the hallway.

As she turned her back to him to open the closet doors, she was aware of his gaze on her. His intense blue eyes tracked her every move, and she felt it to her core. Maybe this was a bad idea.

"I've got one more box of stuff down in my car," he told her, moving toward the door. "That closet should be perfect for my hockey gear. And I promise, I have enough air freshener things to keep it from overpowering the apartment."

"It's all right if you don't," Sasha said with a smile, and she hurried past him into the kitchen and pulled something from a plastic bag. "I got a bulk pack of these plug-in things, and there's an outlet right there by the door. Should keep the hockey boy smell under control."

"Perfect. I'll be right back."

***

Fox leaned against the front door. He squeezed his eyes shut, but he kept seeing Sasha in those tight yoga pants. Maybe this was a mistake.

He needed to get his shit together. He'd had to deal with random chub around Sasha since he'd hit puberty, so this was a familiar struggle. Usually he let his charm and his dick do the talking. But she was his only female friend. And she was important to him. He didn't want things to change.

Sasha developing her tits and ass when they were teenagers had caused him endless hours of torture. So many damn wet dreams. But he knew their friendship was special. Even he wasn't dumb enough to fuck that up. But there were moments when she caught him unaware. Like he had been moments before... The curve of her ass and the subtle arching of her back... His dick throbbed in his jeans. *Damn it.* He needed to get this shit under control. He ran his hands through his hair.

He stepped out into the parking lot, and the wave of humid air calmed the rush in his bloodstream. He would have to be more careful and guarded than he was used to being. It was so easy to let go of himself when he was around Sasha. He'd have to remember he couldn't let go entirely.

He would keep it together most of the time. But he couldn't control his subconscious, so he knew there was no way around the dreams of her that occasionally crept in. The shower had been his undoing. The water soaking through that bra of hers so that her nipples stood out. The way the water streamed between her breasts, trickling down to her navel and into her wet panties— *Fuck.*

Nope. He pushed the memory of her hands rubbing his bare chest and abdomen from his mind. He tried to focus on how pathetic he was, sitting in his soggy underwear, close to tears. Sasha had seen him through a lot, and he didn't want to be just another guy who couldn't appreciate her beyond her body. He didn't want to be another guy who was only interested in getting between her legs. No matter how interested he truly was. They were going to stay friends. He knew he was a player. Thinking of the kind of girls he'd slept with reminded him that he needed to keep his mitts off Sasha. He didn't deserve her.

He needed to get laid. It was always easier to master the mind-over-matter thing when he'd hooked up with a girl. But most of the time, he'd been too focused on hockey to worry about his social life. He didn't need a girlfriend though, just a quick fuck and he'd be back in control of himself. And he wouldn't keep looking at Sasha and thinking about how soft she was to touch and why the fuck she smelled so good.

He glanced down at his dick to ascertain how noticeable his erection would be if he headed back upstairs. Ten minutes in the bathroom and he'd be all right until he could go out and get himself laid. He started running through the list of friends he could call to act as his wingman, but most of them were the guys who had pissed him off during their disastrous dinner at the restaurant.

He shook his head and lifted the box. It was heavy, and the awkward stance he had to adopt to carry it was perfect for concealing his uncooperative dick. He'd figure something out after he had done a bit of unpacking.

He had to see about the list of common courtesy rules Sasha had drawn up, but he had a feeling that bringing a girl home could be the perfect way to convey that he was serious about the two of them remaining friends and roommates but nothing more. Fox was sure he and Sasha were on the same page as far as not wanting to do anything to jeopardize their friendship.

He was unable to knock on the door with anything other than his forehead, earning him an amused eye roll from Sasha when she opened the door. His cock throbbed again as he pushed past her to dump the box of stuff in the corner of the living room.

"So, hear me out. I know me moving in here and helping with the rent and food and stuff is going to help you out with paying for school while your internship is still a for-credit thing. But your job at the restaurant…do you really get enough hours to make enough in tips to cover everything else you need financially?" he asked.

"Um…yeah, sure. I don't hate it at the restaurant, but it's not the kind of job I've *dreamed* of." Sasha played along. "Not exactly a huge secret."

"It's just that I was thinking about this thing Echo was talking about when she came for family dinner last week. She's working on creating and establishing her clothing brand...line..." He paused as he sorted through a stack of DVDs to put them in the empty space on the shelf with Sasha's—there were several duplicates between the two of them, so he put his copies back into the box. "I'm not sure what the difference is?"

"Was there a point to this?" Sasha bent over to open up a box of Fox's stuff labeled 'bathroom.' Her oversized tank top dipped in the front as she bent at the waist, and he could see down the front of her shirt to where her breasts swelled, rising above the dark fabric of her bra as she pulled out his bath towels and carried them to the linen closet.

"Uh...no, I mean yeah," he cleared his throat. He snapped out of his daze before shifting into an awkward crouch by his electronics box, pulling out and sorting his games and books as well as the miscellaneous intertwined power cords.

Peeking over his shoulder to be sure she hadn't come back into the room, he dragged in deep breaths. He could do this. Mind over matter.

"She needs models to work with, and I was thinking she might be interested in working with you. And I knew you could use the money so...what d'you think? Is it something you'd be interested in looking into?"

Sasha shook her head. "C'mon Fox, modeling? I want to be taken seriously."

"What?"

He watched the tilt of Sasha's head shift from leaning toward the left to leaning toward the right. Her eyes narrowed and she jutted her jaw out a bit before clenching her teeth.

"Look, I'm just thinking of what might help. I don't even think of you that way. Like a piece of meat. I mean, I'm not even looking at you as a girl."

She blinked. "You don't?" Sasha asked with a note of disbelief and something else...disappointment?

Fuck. "I mean...it's not like I don't look at you and *see* that you're gorgeous and...stuff." His dick twitched. He turned and paced, hoping she couldn't see just how he thought about her. "Let me try this again. Echo is looking for women she can work with while she's developing her brand. She can't afford, and doesn't really want, traditional fashion models. It's an athletic line, and she was complaining about how regular models' proportions just...aren't right for her...aesthetic...or something like that. She needs *women*, not models. And she wants women who can do more than *just* model. She needs...how did she put it? 'Brand ambassadors,' that was it."

He chanced a glance at Sasha to see if he'd successfully dug himself out of the hole he'd inadvertently stumbled into. Her brow was still furrowed with displeasure, but she no longer looked like she wanted to run his head through the drywall behind the sofa.

"Just meet with her. Call her, have lunch or something. She'll do a way better job of explaining it than I can, I promise you that." He assured her. "And it's not something where you'll be prancing around in your bra and panties as some…male fantasy. You know Echo. Do you really think *that's* the kind of branding she's going for?"

A hint of a smile played at the corners of Sasha's mouth. "I'll *think* about it. I mean, I have a schedule, and it might not fit anyway, so…it will all probably be moot. My work at the station takes priority. But we'll see."

"That's the spirit. And for the record, I don't think it will hurt your chances of getting on camera if people are already familiar with who you are and are used to seeing you. I know you're concerned, but *I* don't think something like this would undermine your career as much as you think it will."

Fox shifted his position as he headed for the bathroom. He just needed a minute. He reached the door, but before closing it, he leaned his head into the hallway. The doorframe conveniently blocked her view. "You know. The guys who tell you how hot you are, I mean, you're all right—" he grinned. That's right, keep it casual "—but I think some of their compliments were strictly part of their attempts to undermine you so they'd find you less threatening. *I*, on the other hand, don't find you threatening at all."

Sasha grabbed a small pillow off the sofa and lobbed it down the hall at his head with a frustrated smirk on her face. He pulled himself into the bathroom and closed and locked the door, leaning back against it as he dragged in deep breaths. In a flash, he had the shower on and his clothes off. Once he was under the water, he began stroking himself. Remembering the way Sasha's touch felt as she'd trailed her fingers up and down his bare back...over his shoulder with the wash cloth...her hand on his knee...then thigh...

As his release snaked through him like lightning, Fox knew he'd be taking a lot of showers.

***

Sasha refused to call Echo for several days. She spoke with her manager at the restaurant about her hours, trying to squeeze in as many as she could between her classes and her internship. But even with Fox helping with the rent, she still had her school expenses to pay for, and *that* bill… Well, there was no way she could make the payment before the deadline unless she took out another loan or found a better job.

She was so close to graduating, but she already had more student loans than she wanted, thanks to her father's refusal to pay for any of her school expenses.

"I'm not taking the money out of your wedding fund," he'd told her when she approached him on the subject.

"You know most parents set those things up the other way around," she'd argued, disgusted by the conversation. "Most parents make a college fund for their kids, and then if the kid *doesn't* go they put it toward things like a car or a wedding. I don't *want* to get married right now or anytime soon. I'm not even seeing anyone!"

But he'd been adamant, and she was now staring at the large bill due in just a few weeks. She swallowed her pride and called Echo during a break between classes to see how much of what Fox had said was true. Sasha had her principles, but at the same time, she did have bills to pay. She trusted Echo's judgment and was confident that whatever

she had in mind would be better than taking out
another loan. She could stomach making money off
her looks to support herself temporarily a little
better than using her looks to marry rich, like her
father wanted.

"Fox told you about it?" Echo asked with
evident surprise. "I didn't think he was even paying
attention."

"Oh, yeah. He does that a lot. Gets that blank
look on his face, and you're pretty sure he's
picturing himself in the net with about fifteen guys
bearing down on him. And then three days later,
whatever you were talking about comes up again
and he winds up repeating word-for-word what
you'd said before," Sasha laughed. "It's creepy."

"Oh, my God, you're right!" Echo admitted
with a laugh. "So, wait, you're interested in working
with me?"

"He said something about maybe I'd be able
to work with you instead of working at the
restaurant, and that you didn't want to shell out the
big bucks for professional models. I'm hoping you
might be willing to hire amateurs like me…" her
voice trailed off. She prayed Echo would pick up on
her hints about being paid without making her beg
for money aloud.

"Well, it sounds pretty perfect to me. I'm still

getting used to the whole hiring people to work for me thing, and interviewing candidates for something like this is just…awkward. What do you say when you want to tell a woman no, and she's a model?" Echo sighed. "But you're definitely more the body type we need, and I'd be so much more comfortable working with you than some of these high-maintenance professionals."

"Great. Just…I don't know…send me a schedule and the kinds of things you'd need me to do for…prep or whatever. I'll try to work my internship around whatever you need," Sasha offered.

"Perfect. I've got Jen coming in to help in a few days…Tuesday, actually. Will that work for you?"

"I get out of class at eleven…" Sasha hoped that wouldn't be too late.

"That'll work! We can get together for lunch first and discuss things. It's a business expense, so don't worry, the meal will be on me. And then after that we can get you in the studio and trying things on, take some demo shots, so I can make a few tweaks before setting up a formal shoot. And we'll discuss compensation."

Sasha breathed a sigh of relief. "That's amazing, Echo. Thank you so much for the opportunity. I'll see you on Tuesday." Sasha hung up, breathing a sigh of relief. This was going to work. Having Fox around was already changing her life.

***

Later that night, Fox hung with Sasha at the house. When was the last time they had done this? Fox lounged back on Sasha's couch, a giant bowl of popcorn between the two of them. He glanced over at Sasha and grinned. This was the first time he had felt normal in weeks. Since the trials.

His chest tightened every time he thought about the way he had blown it. The chance he'd had; it had slipped through his fingers like running water. It made him want to scream. He wasn't going to think about that today, though. He was just going to enjoy veg time.

Before he knew it, a piece of popcorn bounced off his nose. "What the hell was that for?"

"That's for ignoring me when I asked you to pass me a soda."

He frowned. "You asked something? Sorry."

He reached to his side for the cooler and grabbed her a Diet Pepsi. He knew how much she hated Diet Coke. Before handing it to her, he wiped the condensation from the can.

"Fox Coulter, at your service."

Sasha glanced over. "Are you okay?"

He nodded. "Well, as much as a guy who's about to watch a romantic comedy can be."

"Oh, don't pout. You lost the coin toss fair and square. I get to pick the genre." She smirked. "Besides, I know you secretly love these."

The slight flush crept up his neck. See, that was the problem with living with your best friend. And when your best friend was a girl. She knew those things. Those *embarrassing* things. Things she would happily blurt out to some date you brought by.

"I do not."

"Oh yes you do! I still remember you tearing up a little bit at the end of *Love Actually*."

He groaned. "But that was a *good* movie. C'mon Sasha, he was in love with her. He was tortured. He knew he couldn't have her, because she was his best friend's girl."

Sasha laughed. "See, you love these."

"Fine," he crossed his arms. "I've got nothing to hide."

As the movie started and the ridiculously-good-looking-but-funny Hugo fumbled his way into asking out the girl of his dreams, Fox's gaze lingered over Sasha. She sat with her knees to her chest, occasionally dipping her hand into the popcorn. He noticed the tank top and short shorts that she had thrown on when she got home. The shorts were so short that Fox was pretty sure he'd see her ass any second. Not that he was complaining in the least. Her breasts bobbled every time she moved, giving him all sorts of ideas. Torture. Pure torture.

Stop it, best friend. Remember, no more inappropriate thoughts about bestie, got it?

He held onto that thought. He turned his head back to the screen just in time to see the hero and the heroine kissing, like really kissing. It was the kind of kiss that he sometimes wondered about giving Sasha.

No. The kind of kiss you give your dates. You don't kiss your best friend.

He was right. What the hell was wrong with him? Before he'd moved in, his thoughts about Sasha were once in a blue moon. Now they happened daily. It had to be the proximity.

Yeah, keep telling yourself that.

Next to him, Sasha groaned. "On second thought, maybe this movie wasn't the best idea."

He shrugged. "It's not so bad. I was kind of getting into it."

"No, it's great. I actually love this movie. It just reminds me that I haven't had an orgasm in, what, five months? Even longer since I've been kissed like that."

He coughed. "What the hell?" She couldn't be serious.

She shrugged and rolled her eyes. "Yeah, tell me about it." She turned her whole body toward him as she explained. "I mean the kissing thing is almost worse, because at least with Battery Operated Boyfriend I can get an orgasm. But the kissing...man, I miss that. You know that kind of kiss that you sink into. The ones you take your time with, even though you aren't sure if the person likes you or not. There's a little bit of anxiety and anticipation, but you want the kiss to last forever." She took a breath. "You know, the kind that makes your toes curl and your senses singe with heat. I miss those. Ryan didn't like to kiss."

Fox threw up his hands. "Who doesn't like to kiss?"

"Apparently, Ryan. He said that French kissing weirded him out. That it was unsanitary."

Fox glared at her. "Are you fucking serious? I mean, the orgasms, the dude should be shot for that alone. I mean, how do you have a girl like you and not give her constant orgasms. But the kissing thing, that should be criminal. How long has it been since you've been kissed?"

Sasha blushed and darted her eyes down to the bowl of popcorn. "Let's see, we started dating about thirteen months ago. So yeah, thirteen months."

Fox gawked. His eyes wide, mouth open, the whole bit. "You're telling me he never kissed you? You're Sasha Tenison. I know guys to this day that would give their left nut to kiss you. I'd be damned if *I* had you and didn't kiss you."

Sasha laughed. "Now I know you're just trying to make me feel better. But it's true. He loved sex, of course, and wanted plenty of it, but he just wouldn't kiss me."

Fox couldn't believe it. *With lips like hers? They always looked so plump, almost too full for her face, but matched her features perfectly. She looks like one of those Bratz Dolls. Minus the slutty clothing, of course. Stop it.* This is Sasha, but that guy was a moron.

Where did all that come from? Probably from the same place that offered up those inappropriate thoughts about her. The same place the devil lived, and Fox didn't need to go there.

"Sash, he's a moron. Any guy in his right mind would give anything they could to kiss you. Especially if they were dating you. Kissing's half the fun." Fox shook his head. "I mean, not that I want the details mind you, but how did foreplay work?"

Sasha blushed. "Well, he'd start kissing my neck. That part I didn't mind. And obviously—" She looked at her chest and pointed to the parts of herself that Fox swore a mere three minutes ago he would never look at again. And now she was dragging his attention right back to the most perfect pair of tits he'd ever seen. Like a fool, he couldn't help but look.

"Okay, yeah, I don't want to know about that."

Sasha laughed. "Yeah. So I underestimated how watching a romantic comedy would make me feel, especially with all the kissing. I miss it."

Fox gave her another glance. "Yeah, I can imagine. That's just—crazy."

They continued to watch the movie, but Fox's attention was elsewhere. He kept trying to figure out how someone as gorgeous as Sasha could go a year without being kissed. When another scene came on, she groaned. This scene was worse. This scene was leading up to more than just kissing.

"We can watch something else if you want," Fox offered.

"No, it's fine. You know, maybe I'm just going to go hang in my room. Read or something. It's my first night off in a while, and I'm ruining it. I need to just relax."

She set aside the popcorn, but before she could stand, Fox reached out his hand and wrapped it around her wrist. "Sasha, wait."

What the hell was he doing? Although he was fully aware, he couldn't believe what he was about to say. "You deserve someone to kiss you. It's really shitty that Ryan refused to."

"Thanks, Fox. It's my stupid choice for staying with him for so long. I mean, that's just weird, right? No kissing, that's ridiculous."

He nodded. "Yes, it's ridiculous. I'll kiss you." The words tumbled out before he could chicken out.

Sasha's mouth fell open. "What?"

Did he actually say that out loud? There's only one thing to do in a scenario like this. Double down.

Fox shrugged. "Yeah, look, we're friends, so obviously none of this means anything. Plus, you need to be kissed, to be reminded that the douchesac and his hangups aren't you. You didn't do anything wrong in this scenario except stay with him for too long. I'm actually pretty good at it, and I'll be sure to make your toes curl."

She stared at him for a long second. "Wouldn't that be weird? We're best friends."

Fox shook his head. "Nope. Just look at it as an exercise and a chance to practice. You can practice on me, rather than the next guy."

She gasped. "Oh, my God, you might be right. I've been so used to doing it Ryan's way for so long. It will take a while to get back into the swing of things."

He nodded sagely. "Hence, I'm offering you my services. That guy was a dumbass. You deserve someone who kisses you."

She swallowed visibly. "And this isn't weird for you at all?"

Fox shook his head. "Nope." *Liar.*

"So how does this work? Are you gonna stand up and kiss me? That's bizarre."

Fox's heart thumped rapidly against his rib cage, and he feared that the thing would burst. He tried to stay calm by drawing slow, even breaths. "No, just come sit by me. Watch the movie. We'll just chill out and let it happen naturally like it should. Like it does for people everyday."

For a moment he thought she wouldn't go along. He thought she'd walk away. But she eventually sat next to him with the popcorn bowl acting as a barrier.

Fox set the popcorn on the other side of his feet and then pulled Sasha closer to him. "Relax, it's just a kiss. C'mon, how long have we known each other? You're not dating anyone right now, and I'm clearly not looking for a girlfriend. I just think it's a travesty that no one has kissed you in over a year. This is a friend thing." The hell it was. He was desperate to taste her.

Sasha nodded as if what he had said made total sense. That was astonishing, because he had no idea what he was talking about. He hugged her tight to him like he normally did. She eventually leaned against him, her body melting into his. Their shared warmth created an impenetrable cocoon.

They watched the movie for a few more minutes, Fox with his arm around her, casually stroking her shoulder. He was so aware of her. Her apple-scented shampoo, the fine strands of her dark hair almost dancing on his fingertips. He watched her breathing. At this point in the movie, the hero had swung his girl around before planting another kiss on her. Fox leaned over, Sasha looking up expectantly. First her glance was questioning, but then it morphed into curiosity.

Fox angled his head, even as his fingertips still played in her hair. He shifted his other hand to her face, cradling it to remind her that this was him. She could trust him.

This is just a kiss. Fox's thoughts swirled in his head. *Liar.*

He gently brushed his lips to hers. There was an immediate spark.

What the hell?

Instead of pulling back, Fox chased that spark. Sasha parted her lips in a gasp, his tongue sliding into the warm depth of her mouth. His tongue asking hers to play. She stroked her tongue against his, and he moaned. He couldn't help it. He deepened the kiss while his hand slid from her jaw into her hair.

Sasha reached up, her arms winding around his neck. Her fingers teased the hair at his nape.

Oh, hell, Fox thought. *This was not supposed to* —

Sasha arched her back into the kiss, pressing her breasts firmly against his body, and Fox lost total control as he continued to chase the spark as if it were pulling her further and further into him. He dove headfirst into the abyss.

The two of them had just entered completely uncharted territory. It started from something silly. Now it was all too serious. He leaned her backwards, both of them shifting and sliding until she lay along the length of the couch, Fox over her, his hips nestled between her thighs. His lips never leaving hers.

His cock rested against her burning heat as he pressed against her, begging her to let him in. His mind sought any remaining shred of control, but it was long gone. Sasha, his best friend, tasted fucking incredible. He couldn't help but gently rock his hips against her, and what do you know, Sasha widened her legs to give him more room.

He held himself slightly above her, so as to not crush her with his full weight. All the while she rocked her hips up, seeking more of him, and he couldn't help himself. In the matter of a minute they had gone from friendly kissing to desperately pawing at each other. He slipped his hand under her tank top.

She's so damn soft. I just want a taste of her belly button, and up along the bottom of her ribcage.

Sasha arched up as if inviting him. *God, yes.* He wanted to slide his hand up farther still, cupping her fullness in his palm. He wanted to see how well they fit together. The thought had been clawing at him for so long. The alarm bells blared, but the devil on his shoulder just shouted over the din. *Go on. Cup her. You know you want to. She wants it too. She wants your hands on her. Your thumbs on her nipple.* But somehow rationality prevailed, and he just

barely managed to keep from sliding his palm up
over her full curves.

It took his lips longer to get the memo
though. When they finally did, they staged a small
mutiny before he dragged them away from hers as
gently as he could. He kissed along her jaw-line and
had to force himself to sit up and back away…all
the way over to the far side of the couch. Whatever
the hell had happened here was very dangerous.
Destructive.

He couldn't live without Sasha, he needed
her like he needed to breathe. He knew what he was
like, so he wasn't going to ruin this by taking it to a
point of no return. He took her hand and tugged her
into a sitting position.

"Now that's how that dipshit should have
been kissing you." he said before settling back
against the couch like she hadn't just rocked his
whole world upside down.

Chapter Seven

After meeting with Echo on Tuesday, Sasha put in her notice at the restaurant. Echo was going to pay her three times what she made in tips, for a fraction of the work.

"The manager said that I didn't even have to come in for my shifts the rest of the week," she told Fox. "I'm not sure whether to be relieved or insulted." She joined him on the couch, careful not to touch him.

"Well, congratulations on your newfound freedom from the food service industry," Fox mumbled as she munched on her salad. She expected it to be a late night at the station, so she figured dinner at home was prudent. Besides, she liked hanging at home these days.

"I've got a night off on Friday," he said. "Practice will be over by five, at the latest. So what do you say we go out to celebrate? I desperately need to, uh…find some company, if you know what I mean."

She blinked. When she finally computed that Fox might be bringing some bottle blonde back to the apartment, she swallowed hard. "Um…yeah, I know what you mean." She didn't. She liked their bubble. "And…sure, I guess. I should be able to get out of work at the station in time for a night out," she said with a shrug as she had a sudden urge to hunt down her shoes.

In reality, she needed a second to sort through her feelings. "Actually," she said. "It will kind of work out perfectly. There's this after-work thing on Friday that I've been dreading. If I have plans with you I can get out of it, and I won't have to see Ryan. Hanging with you would be a much better start to the weekend. And hey, maybe I can find a hot guy, too. I don't have time for a relationship, but I wouldn't mind flirting a little. It would be nice to talk to someone who actually saw me, you know?"

She slid her gaze over to Fox, who was staring at his phone, jaw slack.

"Fox? Are you okay? Did something happen?" She found the shoe and sat next to him to slip it on, taking the chance to peer at his phone.

"I, uh...I have a voicemail from Coach Tremblay," Fox murmured.

"What did he say?"

"I haven't listened to it yet."

"Well, go on, then." Sasha tucked her feet up onto the seat beside her.

His hands visibly shook, as he took a deep breath and punched in his voicemail retrieval codes.

"Looks like Rhodes is retiring." Coach started. "We're working with the team's publicity staff to draft a statement, and the team has been pushing for more time to prep Henri. In the meantime, however, we're going with the excuse of having to break in the new guy to cover for Rhodes until the announcement."

Sasha held her breath as they listened.

"We'll also be needing a new backup brought up, so you'll have some time to show us what you can do with the rest of the team. Give me a call back, and I'll give you more of the details for the upcoming practice and game schedules. We'll send the paperwork to your agent."

Fox sat stock-still, dazed and unmoving. Sasha grabbed him by the shoulders.

"This is fantastic! Congratulations!" She threw her arms around him. For one brief moment, they sat like that, Sasha pouring all her joy into the hug and Fox holding her close, his big body engulfing hers. Like the night they'd kissed, something bloomed low in her belly, and she ached for something...more. She wanted more of this. *Stop it. Fox Coulter is not on the menu. You'll only get hurt.* And unlike any past boyfriends, the pain would be intense when Fox decided he was tired of her.

"I... That...wasn't what I was expecting," he

managed to mumble while Sasha shook him in her excitement.

"Call him back, call him back," she chanted as she danced on the balls of her feet. "I've got to go finish putting my stuff together and get in to the station, but call me as soon as you talk to him. I want to know everything!"

Fox only continued staring at the phone. "I fucking made it."

She grinned. "You fucking made it." She nodded exuberantly. "You can say it now."

He blinked at her and frowned. "Say what?"

"You were right, Sasha."

A smile cracked through and suddenly, she had the fun-loving Fox back. "The hell I will." But still, he picked her up and swung her around. "I fucking made it."

"Yes, yes you did. And tonight, we celebrate."

***

Sasha hummed the whole way into the station. She'd been worried after the night he'd shown up at her place. But this opportunity would certainly help snap him out of his funk. Now, all he had to do was believe in himself. Easier said than done.

"You look like you're in a good mood,"

Jeanine, her desk mate, said as Sasha dropped her things on her desk. "Good news on your story?"

Sasha deflated a little. "That's...coming along, but no. The news is actually more on personal front. I got a better part-time gig so I was able to quit the restaurant. And my friend, Fox...he *might* have gotten a promotion. I'm waiting for him to call me with the details after he talks to his new boss."

"Wait, Fox? The hot one? Isn't he your roommate now?" Jeanine asked, her curiosity taking over. "You guys keeping things platonic or is it, er, *not an issue?*"

Sasha frowned, then a laugh burst forth. "He's not gay," Sasha said with a roll of her eyes. "And yes on the platonic thing. We've known each other since we were kids, so...we're more like...siblings, I guess...maybe cousins. Anyway, now we have two things to celebrate when we go out on Friday night." Never mind that the man could deliver a panty-melting kiss.

"But Friday we've got that—"

"The thing is, with Fox's work schedule I don't know that it'll be easy for him to change plans like that. I'll have to let you guys know on Friday, but I probably won't be able to go after all."

Jeanine eyed Sasha with a sly grin. "If you're

doing all this to avoid Ryan, I can't say that I blame you," she whispered. "You're well rid of him. The guy's a tool."

Sasha wondered just how many of her friends believed that.

She snapped open her laptop and got to work. There were several messages on her machine from agents and players directly, whom she'd approached about being interviewed for her story.

It took her several hours to call them all back, but by the time she was done, she felt like she had a solid lineup for her piece. She had also received a list of leads for psychologists to approach, for both on-camera interviews and explanations of the various studies she had printed and stacked on her desk next to a pack of highlighters.

Fox called at lunch to give her an update. "I took it," he told her. "I have to go in this afternoon to sign some stuff, but they're working on making up some jerseys for me now."

"That's fantastic!" Sasha exclaimed. But she knew him well enough to check his mood. No one wanted to be second-best. "How're *you* feeling about it? Still excited?"

Some of his earlier exuberance had faded. "I'm all right, I guess. I don't know that it'll really sink in until I get out there on the ice, you know?

Kind of in shock still."

"Have you called your parents yet?"

That one beat of silence told her everything. "No, you're the only one who knows so far. And the team people, obviously. I was kind of putting off telling them. The team doesn't want it getting out before they make their official statement."

And you're afraid it could go away. She knew him well. "Of course. My lips are sealed," she told him, and though she knew he couldn't see it, she mimed locking them and throwing away the key.

"So this whole thing means that my game and practice schedule has changed, and I won't be able to go out and celebrate your dumping the restaurant on Friday night," he said.

"Well…when are you free? I'll make my schedule work around yours. It's a lot easier for me to do that now," she said. "And we need to celebrate your gig, too! A night on the town before your new responsibilities remove you from the pleasures of my company."

"I've really only got tonight. They're making the announcement tomorrow at noon, and I have to be on the bench for tomorrow night's game. I'm slated to make my first start on Friday or Saturday, depending on how Henri does tomorrow night. They don't want to make him do the back-to-back games on the weekend."

"Tonight should be fine," Sasha insisted. "I'll swing by the apartment to change, and we can head out."

"Sounds like a plan," he said. Sasha could sense the lack of enthusiasm in his voice.

"Hey," she said before he could hang up, "you sure you're okay? Given how upset you were about not getting the bump when your friends did…I thought you'd be more excited."

"I…" His voice was quiet. "They didn't want me before because I wasn't good enough. It hasn't even been three weeks since they said that. So I know they're not calling me up because my playing's improved. They don't have a choice, and now…the preseason's almost over at this point, and if I *do* fuck up, it won't just be in games that have no bearing on the standings. It'll be when people are watching and caring and…" He sighed again. "I don't want to screw this up, but I'm not sure I know how *not* to."

"What you need is a distraction and an ego boost," Sasha asserted. "And nothing will accomplish that quite like a night out and getting laid. I promise I will find you someone to hit up that will help you loosen up and get your nerves worked out. I am the best wingwoman ever. Remember

Carly Kincaid?"

Fox laughed. "That woman almost killed me."

True. Carly had been older. And when Sasha had hooked the two of them up, she had no idea just how kinky Carly was. Fox hadn't seemed to mind at the time, though.

"You be my wingman, and I'll be yours, all right? We'll hook each other up," he suggested.

But what if all I want is for you to kiss me again? "Deal. Now I've got to get back to work. Thanks for letting me know what's up. And Fox? Congratulations. You deserve this."

"Thanks, Sash. I'll see you tonight."

She hung up the phone and turned her attention back to the story she was working on, the list of psychologists still on top of the pile of studies. A flicker of guilt sprang up in her chest. She tried smothering it with the fact that Fox had gotten his shot, after all. That he could and *would* succeed. *He's only the inspiration. It'll be fine.* But still, guilt ate at her.

And Fox hadn't proven himself yet, plus his fear of choking was not just real but reasonable. *She* knew he could do it, but if he couldn't get out of his own head he might become a self-fulfilling prophecy. She started thumbing through the stack of studies to see if any of them dealt with cases like Fox's where the athletes were finally granted the all-important opportunity after years of choking. Locating one that looked promising, she pulled it free, uncapped her highlighter, and sat back to read. Maybe she could find a way to help him.

***

It turned out that Tuesday nights weren't particularly popular at the clubs in Pacific Beach. The atmosphere at the places they chose felt distinctly hollow, so after a few dances with each other on nearly empty dance floors, they had gone to a smaller, local place and taken up seats at the bar.

"What about one of those two guys?" Fox said with a nod to the other end of the bar where two Dude Bros watched Sasha with obvious interest.

"I have the distinct impression that if I approached either of them, they'd mention something about a threesome," she snorted. "If they don't already think you and I are together, I doubt they'd object to sharing me. Which, shudder."

He winced. "So…no?"

"No," she answered more firmly, popping a

peanut from the little dish on the bar top into her mouth. "What about her, over there?" Sasha made a suggestion, pointing with an elbow to a woman whose gaze refused to settle on anyone in particular but passed over Fox and Sasha several times. "You should go see if she's waiting for someone. Oh, offer to let her come sit with us if she wants to avoid getting unwanted attention from those assholes over there," she pressed.

"Won't she think you and I are together?"

"Maybe, but if you tactfully get up to go to the bathroom or make a call or something, I'll tell her the wingman deal. I'll let her know how sweet you are or some crap like that. Or you can tell her you'll sit with her while she waits for her boyfriend, or friends, or whoever she's waiting for. Be innocuous and don't press. Be a nice guy."

Fox rolled his eyes but rose from his seat and left to chat with the other woman. "I have done this before, you know." A few short minutes after he walked away, the two guys who'd been watching her strolled over and took up seats on either side of her.

"Let us buy you a drink," Thing One said to start, signaling the bartender to come over.

"I'll drink if you want to pay, but I'm telling you now that I'm not interested in anything beyond that." *At least, not with either of you.* She wanted to tack onto the end.

"That's fine," Thing Two said with a tone that made Sasha's skin crawl. "We know you came in with someone else. He your boyfriend? Did you two have a fight?"

"What'll it be?" the bartender asked, his eyes watching the two men who cradled her.

"Long Island iced tea," she ordered. "On one of these guy's tabs."

The men didn't press her until after the bartender had gotten her the drink and moved farther along the bar.

"Still haven't answered about whether that guy you came in with is your boyfriend or not," one of them pointed out.

"Nope." She left it at that.

"Looking for one? Pretty girl like you should have a boyfriend," the man on her left inquired.

She smiled beatifically. "Sorry, dude. You're not in the running." *Because you're not Fox.*

***

Fuck, he was rusty when it came to normal girls. For the last year, he'd just hooked up with the girls that hung around the rink. Those girls didn't require much conversation. Easy and available.

He quickly put the woman Sasha had singled out for him at ease by assuring her he was only there to give his friend some space.

"Oh," she said. "Too bad. You're cute. I'm just waiting for some of my friends anyway, but I had the time we were supposed to meet wrong," she confessed. "I'm actually seeing someone."

Fanfuckingtastic.

"Congratulations," Fox muttered, turning his attention back to Sasha as the two men who'd been watching her settled in on either side of her. Her shoulders went tense. He had to keep reminding himself that Sasha could take care of herself. And that he could move quickly if either of those goons did something she didn't want or like.

"You like her," his companion remarked after a few moments. "Don't you?"

Fox cleared his throat and flushed. "I, uh — What makes you say so?"

"Thought so," she said with a laugh. "Why don't you just tell her?"

Fox sighed. "She's my best friend. Not gonna fuck that up. Let's just sit here for a minute and pretend we're having a good time and then later I'll make something up about why things didn't work out," he suggested.

The bartender approached a few minutes later with a Long Island iced tea and a message.

"Sir, your friend from over there requested that I only give her the first drink those guys bought, and after that to send the rest down here for the two of you to enjoy," he said discreetly, glancing over his shoulder at Sasha and her two admirers.

"What are you giving her now?" Fox asked while watching Sasha as she continued to sip from her glass, while the men around her looked pleased with themselves.

"Arnold Palmer. She also wanted me to pass this to you." The bartender handed him a folded napkin. Inside, Sasha had scrawled, "Enjoy the free drinks."

Fox rolled his eyes in amusement. "Would you care for the first one?" he offered to the woman beside him, who was thoroughly entertained.

"I've already got my drink," she said, raising her margarita. "That one's for you."

Fox grinned as he tapped the edge of his glass against hers. "Cheers."

***

"Okay, you know what? We'll play a game. You beat me and I'll give you my number, my *real* number. I beat you, you hit the skids and leave me to my drink. What do you say?" Sasha could tell by the look they exchanged, they thought they had this in the bag, had *her* in the bag. It would certainly be fun to dissuade them of that notion.

What they didn't know was that she had been perfecting her darts game in college dive bars for years. It was usually how she got her going-out money.

I'm a hustler, so what? They don't need to know that.

In her peripheral vision, she watched Fox and the pretty girl, trying to ignore the twinge of jealousy. *He's not yours.* She never should have agreed to helping each other get laid. It was dumb, but she'd wanted to celebrate with him. He'd worked so hard, and to be honest, Ryan was right about a few things. Sasha worked too much, almost to the detriment of everything else. She was driven, but outside of work she had no life. It was time to change that.

"C'mon, sweetheart. Are we going to play or what?"

Thing One, the guy on the left, took his turn. He wasn't half bad, so she had to be careful. No way in hell was she actually giving either of these guys her number.

The other guy was worse, *far* worse. He couldn't play for shit. When Sasha took her turn, she gave them both a sickly-sweet smile. One by one, she tossed her darts. She jumped with a squeal of delight, when they all landed in the inner two rings.

"Sorry boys, better luck next time."

Thing One grabbed her arm with so much force that she winced. "You fucking hustling us?"

"If I were you, I'd let her go." Fox's voice was calm but icy.

Was it bad that Sasha felt a tinge of thrill when Fox went off the rails for her? It was sad, because she always stood for feminism and fought for equality. This was the second time she had gotten hot over him fighting for her. It was almost ridiculous.

Although, she did have eyes. With all that lean muscle, those tattoos and his movie star face, added to the fact that he was ready to fight? It was hot, speaking to some primal instinct that had been buried deep inside of her. It was an instinct that couldn't be reasoned with by logic. It was her libido.

Sasha twisted her arm from his grip. "It's okay. These assholes were just leaving."

Thing Two looked as if he wanted to argue, but then tapped his friend's chest while heading for the door.

Fox turned his attention back to her. "I swear, I can't leave you alone for a damn minute. Why is that?"

"You'd miss me too much?" She grinned up at him.

He shook his head while letting out a chuckle. "Maybe."

Sasha planted her hands on her hips. "Well, don't. You have a perfectly cute girl over there. I wouldn't even mind making awkward small talk with her tomorrow morning while you showered. That's saying a lot."

Fox laughed. "What am I going to do with you?"

"Don't ask that. Instead, ask what you are going to do with the cute brunette. She looks like a school teacher, but she might be into super kinky shit, wanting you to tie her up with complicated knots or whatever. I mean, she might let you do anything to her, which has to have some kind of appeal."

"I'm not sure you have any idea of what appeals to me," Fox said quietly.

Sasha was teasing, but the joking suddenly stopped when Fox focused his intense blue eyes onto her lips. Just like that, they were back on the couch, his erection pressing into her just the way she needed it to. He was licking into her mouth, kissing her so deliciously that her body vibrated with need.

She had to break the spell or else she was going to do something that she couldn't take back. She was tempted to wrap herself around him and beg him to do it again.

She cleared her throat. "You'd better get back to her before someone else swoops in."

Fox glanced at the brunette while she waved back at him. "I'm right where I belong."

Chapter Eight

Fox fumbled with the key at the door to their apartment, dropping it on the floor twice before he managed to get it into the lock successfully.

"You should've let me take care of that," Sasha told him in a loud whisper.

"Please," he scoffed as he finally pushed the door open and held it for her to pass him into the apartment. "You practically fell into that cab."

"I can't believe I had so much to drink," she muttered, shuffling toward the kitchen. Then she giggled as she reached up to the cabinet and pulled out the coffee tin, peeling the lid back and taking a deep sniff of the grounds. "God, I need to sober up, or I'll be miserable in the morning."

"You only had three of those things," he reminded her. "I had…four? No…I had three, and the two beers before you started sending those things over to me. And *I'm* supposed to have practice after they make the announcement," Fox told her as he opened the freezer and stuck his head in.

"You can't sleep in there, Fox."

"I'm going to be so hung over at the press conference tomorrow. They're going to put me in front of a bunch of reporters with…flashing lights and…questions." He groaned. "The last thing I need is to do that and have them all realize how hung over I am. That would become my thing then. I'd be the partier or the one who can't handle it and gets drunk. They'll send me back down for sure."

"While you're in the freezer, grab that frozen pizza," Sasha instructed as she filled the coffee pot with water and poured it into the reservoir on top of the machine. Fox set the oven to preheat and pulled out a cooking sheet and aluminum foil. After setting the coffee machine to percolate, Sasha disappeared to the bathroom for a few minutes, leaving Fox to get the pizza into the oven. He hadn't had enough to eat before they started drinking—neither of them had. Getting some food and coffee down would help to sober them up.

"Here you go," Sasha declared, returning with the bottle of aspirin. "Head it off, and we'll be fine in no time. We weren't very successful, were we?" she said before swallowing her own aspirin down with a swig of water. She pulled two mugs from the cabinet and stood in front of the coffee machine as the brew trickled through the filter and into the pot below.

"I wouldn't say that," he objected. "I didn't go home with that girl, but I did have a pretty good time with you. And we were quite successful in securing free alcohol. Or should I say, *you* were successful," Fox said, with a laugh.

"I find it disturbing they weren't deterred by the fact that I flat out told them I wasn't interested. They just kept buying more drinks as though that would change my mind."

"Probably would work on a lot of girls. Luckily, you are *all* woman. They didn't know what to do with you," Fox teased.

"Luckily, I had you there to help keep shit from getting out of hand."

He crossed his arms. "I don't get it, though. Why did you even entertain them?"

"Because I'm out of practice. With everything. My focus has been so single-mindedly on my career and my future that I've put everything else on hold. That kiss from a couple weeks ago... I mean, how had I gone a year without being kissed? And how have I gone months without an orgasm? It's crazy because I *love* sex. I love the connecting and feeling close to someone. I can't sleep with a random guy, though. I need to feel connected to someone in order to sleep with them. I need to like them, or at least respect them."

Fox nodded. "I get that."

How? He didn't even know the women he'd slept with, let alone like them. Lately everything had seemed so…empty. He needed to break this fucking habit. To distract himself, he pulled the pizza out of the oven, sliced it, and served them each a couple of pieces.

"So…what was wrong with the other women in the place?" Sasha said between bites. "What made you come home with me when I struck out?"

"You didn't strike out," he said, turning the focus back on her. "And striking out implies that you were hoping to get a hit, but…you didn't seem too interested in anything like that."

Sasha shrugged and flushed. "There weren't any guys there I found interesting enough to want to go home with. Or to take home. I—I don't *miss* Ryan. I don't miss being in a relationship with him, I don't miss his need for reassurance about everything, his jealousy. But I'm a bit rusty when it comes to the dating thing," she confessed. "I was with him for almost a year, and it was…what it was. But I haven't had to go looking for a guy." She avoided looking at Fox as she said it. "I *want* to be with a guy, but I'm not sure that I'm ready to just pull any guy into bed with me." She sighed.

"I…I get that," Fox admitted. "I haven't put a lot into my social life lately either. Been too focused on hockey to seduce women," he said with a laugh.

"As if *the* Fox Coulter would ever be too busy. We'll just have to push each other to practice more, I guess," Sasha said with a laugh. There was a playfulness in her eyes...and something more. What was that? Was she flirting?

"What exactly do you mean by 'practice'?" he asked. His skin was too hot. Clammy. He was encouraging this. What he wanted to do was touch her. Dig his hands into her hair and kiss her until she couldn't breathe. But then he would be no better than the two assholes at the bar, hoping to get her drunk enough to give into their coaxing. He shoved more pizza into his mouth to keep him from saying more than he should.

She cocked her head at him. "I..." she started but looked away, her face reddening. "I didn't mean...anything by it. Just...never mind."

He frowned, confused. "What are you saying, Sash?"

"I don't know. I think I need practice. Practice dating. Practice kissing. Practice interacting with guys who aren't douchebags. Before Ryan, there was Matt. That was another long-term relationship that I didn't have to do much work for. They were both just there, easygoing. You know, I can't even remember why Matt and I broke up."

Fox could. "He moved to Arizona. Wanted you to go with him."

She frowned, but nodded. "Oh yeah, I just sort of felt *blah* about him, which sounds awful. We dated during the last year of college. He was perfectly nice, lovely. I was just looking for a spark of something that we just didn't have. When he was leaving, it seemed like the perfect time to end it. A couple of months later, I met Ryan. It was fun before his jealousy started to shine through. In so many ways, it was easier being with him than being on my own."

"Why do you think that is, Sash?"

"Honestly, I don't know. Maybe because for my entire life my Dad has told me that I'm basically worthless without a guy. And I bought into it. Even though I rail against that shit every day. I usually think I'll be happy in a relationship, but then I'm not. I want to practice dating, to see what it's really like. I don't need to start a relationship, you know?"

Fox understood. She wanted playfulness, she wanted for things to be easy. She didn't want to *be* with anyone, which was fine by him. He adored Sasha, but he was a man-whore. In no way was he looking to settle down. Not even for her.

"I'm sober enough to know what I'm doing, but not sober enough to care," Sasha whispered."

Fox stared into her eyes and cursed low. She moved to put her empty plate in the sink.

He tried to shift around her to the sink, but she stood with her arms braced against the edge of the counter, blocking his access. He moved to slide past her, but there wasn't much room to maneuver, and he unintentionally brushed against her ass, his cock twitching at the inadvertent contact.

He froze, praying she hadn't noticed, but he knew she must have, given how she stiffened. Should he apologize? Pretend it hadn't happened? She wasn't saying anything, so maybe she was going to pretend nothing had happened, too.

Then she did move. She leaned back, pressing her ass against his crotch so that his cock was caught between the firm curve of her right buttock and his thigh. He was hyperaware of each throbbing pulse, and was certain she could feel it, too.

Should he rock against her? Let her know he was open to…whatever it was she wanted to do? Or should he move himself away from her and keep that safe distance of friendship between them? Yeah, do that one. But shit, he couldn't move. He wanted to be here, with her, the scent of her apple shampoo driving him crazy.

Even if he had truly believed that stepping

away was the smarter thing to do, Fox couldn't control his body's response to Sasha's.

He held his breath as he rocked his hips, gently grinding his cock into her ass. He could easily — and he desperately wanted to — pull her skirt up, her panties down, his jeans down, and slide into her right there against the counter. But there was some sort of balance in what they were doing that he couldn't bring himself to upset.

Fox tried to assess their state of intoxication. He had certainly had more than Sasha, however the food and coffee had gone a long way to removing the effects of what he'd drunk. His head was less fuzzy. Well, it was a different kind of fuzzy. And on top of that, he felt surer on his feet, his stomach had settled down, and so far, there was no sign of a headache.

It would be so much easier to think if he weren't so distracted by the warmth of her ass against his cock and his slipping control.

"How…" he began, then swallowed and tried again, succeeding in sounding less strained the second time. "How drunk do you think you are? How — how are you feeling?"

"I'm not drunk anymore. Just hazy, I guess. I feel liberated."

I'll worry about ramifications tomorrow. Later. So much

later.

Right now he wanted to taste her lips again. He wouldn't think about that niggling voice in the back of his mind that screamed at him, *Sasha is so much more than this.* He wasn't going to listen to that voice. Because that voice would keep him from getting too close. Gently, he turned her in his arms, and placed his mouth on hers.

Home.

The thought horrified him for the briefest of seconds, before sensation swamped him, pleasure pulling him under.

He eventually broke the bond between their mouths and moved his lips along her jaw. Sasha leaned her head back, exposing the column of her throat. Fox kissed her again, then grazed his teeth along the sensitive skin. She shivered when Fox rocked his hips into hers.

Holy fuck. He almost came.

"Fox—"

He slid his arms up her ribcage, chasing rib after rib, until he reached her breasts. The perfect orbs filled his hands, overflowing his palms.

Jesus, she's so soft.

Sasha rocked into him, while his cock throbbed in his jeans, begging for an escape. "Sasha, you sure about this?"

She nodded. "You're my best friend." She said that as if it were an answer, as if it were the only indication that was needed to explain why they were doing this. She rolled her hips against him one more time. Fox stopped caring. They *were* best friends, and he wouldn't hurt her.

But will she hurt you? His mind teased.

As the lust pulsed through his veins, he lost all inhibitions. He wanted her. He wanted her badly, but he wasn't thinking clearly enough. In hindsight, he wished he hadn't had that last drink. But still, they were sobering up fast, as if the lust burned the alcohol from their blood.

He yanked down the straps of her dress, and her bra followed suit. She freed her arms, leaving the cups in place. Fox pulled them down, letting her breasts spill freely into his hands. Her nipples acted as a homing beacon for his fingers, causing him to immediately start tugging gently on them, and rolling them between his thumb and forefinger. Sasha hissed, and Fox turned her so she braced her hands across the sink for leverage.

She was in the perfect position. Fox didn't know how or why, but his hand started up the skirt of her dress. A gorgeous purple thong on the most perfect ass he had ever seen in his life. He wanted to massage it, squeeze it, bite it, *fuck* it.

He gently hooked the elastic waist of her panties over his thumbs, and began sliding the satin fabric down. They slid over her hips, past her ass and then down her long, slim legs, to her knees. Before he could stop himself, he slid his hands up the back of her thighs and cupped her cheeks, her curves molded to his hands.

When he stood again, she was pushing back into his caress. Sasha reached over, grabbing for him. With her hand on his package, she wrapped delicate fingers around him and squeezed, stroking him through his jeans. He was sure he was going to come just from her touching him like this. He kept thinking of that day on the couch, when their kiss had gone from friendly, to possessive, to needy.

When he pressed his cock right against her hot, moist center, he never wanted to leave. She arched her hips, wanting him there. He needed her legs to open wider, so he could seat himself so far inside of her Sasha couldn't tell where she ended and he began.

There was a rustling of clothes. Fox's belt buckle clattered. Once again, they were practically connected at their lips. Their tongues caressing, their teeth nipping at one another like desperate animals.

Fox ran his fingers up her thighs, gripping, and possessive. He then plunged his thumb into her sweet center, stroking her. She was wet, slick, and hot. She was ready.

Soooo damn ready.

With her feet, she pushed his jeans down his legs. Then his boxers. He teased the tip of his cock against her hot center. Fox shuddered while she hissed with pleasure. She widened her legs, allowing him access to more of her.

Holy fuck.

He gripped the base of his shaft, then ran it along her slick center to her clit, then back again. Every time he teased that hot button of nerves, she shuddered and moaned his name. Sasha's hands clutched his shoulders with nails digging into him. She chanted his name. "Fox, Fox, oh my God, Fox. Please, I need you."

Sasha was vocal lover, and shit, he liked that. He liked that a lot. She threw her head back and he leaned over her, attaching his lips to her throat, kissing and nibbling. Suddenly, they weren't just teasing anymore. The tip of his dick pushed just inside of her.

God, it feels so damn – Oh, fuck. Condom.

Sasha lifted her head. "What's wrong?"

Fox held himself as still as he could bear. He didn't want to move, in fear that he was going to blow. Sasha had felt so good. Fuck, she was hot. So tight. Shit. Why was she so tight? He had never had sex without protection, there were so many incredible sensations. The heat and moisture was tempting his cock to go deeper.

"Condom. I don't have a condom. They're in my room."

Sasha moaned, "Fox—I—"

Fox wanted this, he wanted to sink deep inside of her. But he was a good guy, not like one of the assholes that would have just used her and never spoken to her again. He wasn't going to do this, not to Sasha.

"We need to stop. I'll go get the condoms, just wait—"

She wasn't hearing it. "Fox, I'm on the pill."

As if those were the magic words, he slipped a few centimeters further into her. *Shit. I can't.* He had slept with too many women to count. He was beginning to think that it wasn't a good idea. Before he could convince himself to stop, her inner muscles tightened around him, causing him to groan. He slid all the way home, and it was the best thing he had ever felt.

"Sasha, holy hell."

She understood, because she was mumbling, "...so good. Yes, right there. So...Fox...Good."

That was it. They were making love. Fucking, making each other feel so good. He and Sasha, against her kitchen sink. He drove his dick into her, over and over, pulling out till just the tip remained. His hands gripped tightly around her hips, keeping her in position. She wrapped her legs around him, meeting him thrust for thrust. Sasha grabbed at his hair, and before Fox knew it, he was going to blow. Fox didn't know if this would ever happen again.

I want to make this shit last.

With a growl, he stopped them. Sasha whimpered as she rotated her hips into him, begging for more. He slowly disengaged, and she cried against him.

"Shh. I'm not going anywhere. You feel too goddamn good around my dick." Fox gently lifted her feet off the ground again and he turned her so that she faced the sink. With his knee, he nudged her thighs wider apart as she braced herself against the sink. The tip of his cock bumped her folds. He moaned her name as he slid home again.

"Fuck. This is too good. Feels too amazing." He murmured as he leaned over her, wrapping his body around hers, cupping her breasts and gently massaging them.

Sasha groaned low and worked her hips back, even as he drove in deep. She chanted his name, over and over again. "Fox, Fox, Fox." He gently pinched her nipples, added more pressure, and she started to shake. *Oh, hell.*

He liked seeing this. He liked seeing her falling apart for him. He filled her deep, marking her as his.

She's not yours. This is only temporary. A one-time thing, so get your head in the game and enjoy it.

While one hand still cupped and kneaded her breast, his other slid down over her waist to her hip. He squeezed gently, and then Sasha did something he never felt before. Mid-stroke, her walls clamped around him. She wasn't exactly coming, yet. She was doing this on purpose, as if to keep him inside of her.

No way in hell was he going to last longer than a minute if she kept that up. With a hand on her ass, he pulled her ass cheeks apart slightly, so he could watch his cock slide deep inside her wet center.

God damn. I'll never get used to this.

And you won't have to, because you're just a rebound guy.

He was making her feel good. And the better he made her feel, the more likely she'd let him touch her again. Determined to see that happen, Fox reached around the front of her hips, until he found that sweet, slick juncture between her thighs. He knew exactly what to do to send her skyrocketing.

But instead of just pressing her clit, and yanking the orgasm from her, he teased. Oh so gently, his middle finger flickered over her clit, seeking the most sensitive pleasure spot on her body.

Sasha bucked against him. "Oh my God, Fox. Holy shit—" She braced her arms on the sink in front of her and pushed her ass back against him until he was balls-deep. She came hard and fast and cupped his dick so tight that he thought he might never escape.

Not that I want to.

He could die right here and be perfectly happy. He held her hips tight with both hands, sinking in deep, over and over, until she was coming again.

"Fuck, Sasha." Her name was part epithet. She was a goddess, but she had no right to make him feel like this. She had no right to be this hot. No right to be this perfect for him.

His orgasm crashed into hers, and he came hard. Unable to stop himself, he clamped his teeth on the base of her neck and bit gently. Sucking her skin, attempting to consume her, before gently licking over the tender bite with his tongue.

He never wanted to leave. He was going to stay right here until she forced him out. *Don't go getting attached, lover boy. You are the rebound guy.* And for now, that was okay. Sooner or later, she'd look at him the way he'd been looking at her since they were kids.

***

Fox was in trouble. There was no way he was ever going to get enough. He was bound and determined to live out every fantasy he'd ever had about Sasha. And from the looks of it, she'd had a few fantasies, herself.

His fingers rooted in her hair as he rolled to lay her flat on her back, his weight bearing her down into the mattress. His grip was tight as he pulled her head back, breaking the kiss. His eyes searched hers and found only warmth and welcome. She loosened her hold on him, and smoothed his hair back from his forehead and temples. He dropped his face to her neck and placed openmouthed kisses along her neck and collarbone, his hands sliding up to cup her breasts while she lifted her hands above her head.

Sasha giggled when his lips skimmed the tops of her breasts.

Fox traced the petals with his fingers, and her nipples hardened, and her breathing hitched. He bent his head and slid the lace aside to run his tongue over the tight tips, licking her sensitive skin.

Sasha arched her back beneath him and ran her hands over his back, her fingernails lightly raking him when he began using his teeth.

"I'm not hurting you, am I?" he asked as his nose trailed through the valley between her breasts before he repeated the process on the other one, this time, using his teeth to tug the lacy fabric down.

"Not at all," she answered with a smile. Sasha outlined the muscles across his shoulders and arms, then dug her elbows into the mattress to arch her back as Fox's tongue flicked across her nipple.

Before he could continue torturing her, she tugged him back so she could kiss him again. Fox slid his hand over her soft skin, caressing the curve of her hip and thigh before shifting between her legs. Fuck, she was wet. His cock stirred. *Already ready for another go.* Yeah, why not? He'd already crossed into dangerous territory.

He found her slick, wet, and ready, and he groaned against her lips. "Sash, condoms. We should use them. Last time I — " He cleared his throat. "We should use them."

Sasha sat up. "I told you, I'm on the pill. And I'm clean. I got tested right after Ryan."

The relief was immediate. "I swear, Sash. I've never — "

She held his face, gently brushing his cheekbones with her thumbs. "I believe you."

One of her hands trailed down from where she'd been stroking the line of his jaw as they kissed. The muscles of his belly clenched beneath the light graze of her fingernails. Then she began gently but purposefully stroking his cock. *Oh, shit.* One touch from her was all he needed, and he was ready to go.

"I want you." Her voice was low as she tightened her grip. He bent his head to kiss her again, the both of them driving each other crazy. Only the sounds of their moans and groans filled the silence in her bedroom.

She hooked her fingers into his head.

"Fuck, Sasha. Yes. Show me how much you want me."

"Fox, oh, my God. Please — "

Fox hovered above her briefly as Sasha wrapped her legs around his waist, her soft inner thighs gripping him. "Sasha — " he whispered, then drove home. With a kiss, he slid in deep, resting his forehead against hers, as he waited a few beats before starting to move inside her.

This time, they moved together with long, slow strokes. Her hands came to rest near the small of his back, gently urging him back into her each time, her rocking body driving him higher and higher.

Bearing his weight on his elbows, he let his hands tangle in her hair and caress her face. She was so damn beautiful.

Except for a few times when the need to close their eyes and chase a sensation was impossible to ignore, they spent the entire time locked in one another's gaze.

Lightning wrapped around Fox's spine, and the shaking started in his toes. She locked her legs around him, holding him inside her and rolling her hips in time with his. As she came, his lips were on hers, and he let go.

Fox was too spent and content to do anything but lay his head on her breast, hoping he wasn't crushing her with his weight.

Between Sasha stroking his hair and the metronomic rhythm of her heartbeat beneath his ear, Fox was soon lulled to sleep.

Chapter Nine

Fox woke to the feel of Sasha's satin skin all around him. Her body had tucked into his during the night, and her ass gently cradled his cock as she slept. Unbeknownst to him, and likely her, she liked to tease when she was asleep. All night, he'd woken up intermittently to slow gyrations of her hips. It was why he hadn't let her sleep much. Every time he woke up he was hard and ready, and she was naked and wet for him. It was no different now.

Instinctively, he curled his arm around her, wanting to pull her closer. Although she needed sleep, and so did he. He had a damn press conference today. And for once he wasn't nervous. *Nothing like fucking your best friend again to help loosen yourself up.*

He ignored the devil on his shoulder. He was going to let her rest. Because he wasn't sure how she'd feel when she woke up enough to realize the ramifications of what they'd done. He wanted to give her time. Just because Sasha had fueled every teenaged wet dream of his for years, that didn't mean she'd be down for this happening again, and again…and again.

Carefully he slid his arms from around her and rolled out of the bed. He quickly checked the time on her bedside clock. It was 4 a.m. He should go back to sleep, but he had a feeling he wouldn't be able to. He was wide awake now, and seemingly, his dick was in no mood to give him a break.

Something made him pause. He didn't just want to walk out on her. He wanted to stay. He wanted to pull her into his arms, and keep her there.

What the hell was wrong with him? He wasn't into sleepovers. He usually liked his space.

While he was the fun-loving, wisecracking one of his siblings, he was also an introvert. He relished his space and time alone. He preferred it. But with Sasha, he was different. It wasn't uncomfortable. It was painful to leave her there, but still he slipped out of bed and tucked the blanket around her, covering her shoulders so that she'd stay warm, then he padded out into the living room.

He was too keyed up to go to sleep now, and the rink didn't open for at least another hour. Today was the day they'd announce that he was on the team, and it would be too late to go back. Not that he wanted to go back, but still. Instead of lying in Sasha's arms, where he wanted to be, he sat down to watch game film. When it came to games, he knew how to study. Whenever his life turned into chaos, he always returned to the ice. Since he couldn't lace up his skates right now, watching game films was the next best thing.

He focused on this instead of focusing on the woman he'd just left alone in bed. He prayed to God that he hadn't fucked up their friendship. Because at the end of the day, he couldn't have her.

***

Sasha woke about ten minutes before her normally scheduled alarm. She waited for the panic, but it didn't come. She was naked and *alone* in her bed. She sat up, clutching the sheets to her chest, fighting off the fog of sleep to remember... Fox had fallen asleep on top of her. *Inside* of her.

She'd been stroking his hair, and she must have dozed off, herself.

But sometime in the night, he'd woken up and tucked her properly into bed — they'd definitely been on top of the sheets, but his warmth had kept her from feeling chilly. And then he'd left her in bed, *alone*. She squelched the flare of worry. Waking up alone didn't mean anything when it had to do with Fox.

Sasha stretched, relishing the delicious soreness that lingered in her limbs. Muscles she hadn't used in a while made their presence known. She felt good, though. Better than good. Well, she supposed a couple of orgasms would do that to a girl.

But she was worried about seeing Fox again. If he'd stayed in the bed with her and they'd woken up together, that would have been one thing. But to wake up alone…that was something else. Being with him had been better than she'd ever imagined. She hadn't expected to feel so connected to him. Like all he cared about in the world was her.

That first time in the kitchen, that had been raw and desperate. But what happened after… *That* was connection. The whole time he'd been inside her, looking at her…she knew he'd been *seeing* her.

What she wanted to do was crawl back in bed and rewind the clock. Have him back. Instead she sighed as she slipped from the bed and pulled on a pair of pajama bottoms and a tank top. When was the last time she'd had sex that good?

Sex with Ryan had been…selfish. Mostly about him. She didn't believe in faking it, and she'd never had to bother trying because it hadn't concerned him. Usually when he was done, he'd roll away and fall asleep. She admitted to herself that she was *partly* to blame. It could take a while for her to get into things mentally and physically. It had been frustrating for Ryan. Though she hadn't had that problem last night.

With Ryan, there had been a few times when her patience with his fumbling attempts had run out, and she'd pushed him to use lube and get it over with. He'd quickly adopted that attitude in the bedroom, doing away with foreplay, leaving her only moderately satisfied most of the time. It had made her more than willing to put sex off in favor of what she considered more important tasks, like her classwork or assignments for the station.

Gathering her courage to venture outside her bedroom, Sasha promised herself that things with Fox didn't have to change because of what had happened. He had been overwhelmed and on edge with his sudden elevation to the major league team, and in desperate need of something to relieve the tension. *And what was your excuse, other than wanting him?* Alcohol and her own desire for physical intimacy had combined with his need to result in some slightly blurred lines. But they could go back, right? It was only sex. *Only the best sex you've ever had.*

But who said they couldn't step back across that line? She didn't have time for a relationship. And since he was just starting with the team and would have a full schedule of his own, there was no reason they had to turn their night into a big thing. On the contrary. Maybe trying to force it into the kind of relationship that was more than just friendship might be the very thing that would destroy what they had. They were adults. They were friends. They could and would be mature about this. *Except you know what his O face looks like. And he's come inside of you.* God, had he. Four times. Each time, he'd whispered her name on a curse before letting the waves of bliss crash in on them.

She pushed open her bedroom door and crossed to the kitchen. The pot of coffee she'd made the night before, long forgotten. She dumped it into the sink and washed the carafe out so she could brew a fresh batch. As she was pouring the grounds into the filter, Fox emerged from the bathroom, wearing, like her, a T-shirt and pajama bottoms.

"Morning," he said, looking away from her as he

shuffled into the kitchen to grab some cereal from on top of the fridge.

Okay…so he was going to pretend everything was okay?

"Morning," she said with a blush. They'd left the remnants of their pizza on the counter the night before, in their haste to get to the bedroom. She pulled the trash bin out from under the sink, and brushed the half-finished crusts into it.

He cleared his throat. "So, uh…last night was…fun," Fox said before stuffing a spoonful of Corn Flakes into his mouth.

She stood straight, and forced herself to breathe for a full five count before turning to face him.

"I had fun, too," Sasha said. Why was this so awkward? *Because you're not meant to see your best friend naked.* Even if he did have a spectacular body. "It was…good. Great," she blathered. *Oh, real smooth, Sash.*

"Me too," Fox admitted. "It's, uh, worked something out of my system."

She frowned, unsure how to take that. "I slept well after. I didn't even notice you leave."

Did he just wince? "I had to use the bathroom," he told her. "And then when I realized what time it was and how soon I had to get up for practice and that press conference, I didn't want to disturb you. I really wasn't trying to avoid you or anything like that. I wasn't even gone all that long. Like you said, I slept well, too."

His rambling made Sasha relax and laugh. "I know you weren't trying to avoid me," she reassured him. "Look, I think we both know that last night was a one-time thing. It was great, but neither of us has the time right now to try and make it into something…more. I'm super busy with my internship and classes, and now this thing with Echo. You're going to be traveling a lot more for the team, and practicing—"

His eyes narrowed. "Right. Traveling."

Sasha crossed to him and put a hand on his arm, more aware of the feel of him, the swell of his muscle, the tension from holding his bowl of cereal, than she would have been before. "You're going to be great and…busy," she added. "Last night was terrific, like I said, but one time." She breathed deep. "We're okay."

She kissed his cheek and rested her forehead against his cheekbone for a moment. She had to work to ignore the flash of heat in her belly as she recalled the way he'd rested his head against hers as he'd slid into her last night. The pressure of his lips pressing a kiss to her temple distracted her from her thoughts.

"Thanks, Sash."

She smiled at him then, watching him scrunch up his nose.

"By the way," he continued in a whisper, "you might want to hop in the shower when you're done with your coffee. After all, you spent the night having hot, sweaty sex," his voice was hoarse as he teased her.

She pulled back, knowing her face was red, and gave him a playful jab on the arm. "Shut up," was all she could think to respond with. He laughed and went back to eating his cereal. "And what about you? You have to head to the rink soon. Were you planning on showering before you go?"

He answered with his mouth full. "Why? Are you inviting me to join you?" He waggled his eyebrows, but his eyes focused intently on her. Sasha closed her eyes, and pressed her lips together to fight the urge to laugh. "Come on. I know you think that was funny. I'm hilarious, and I know your tells." A chuckle slipped out of her. "See? And, no, I wasn't planning on showering before I leave. I'm just going to get sweaty and gross at practice this morning, and will have to shower before the press conference anyway." He looked up and registered her glare but waved it off, nearly dumping his next spoonful of Corn Flakes onto the floor.

"All right. Well, I'm going to go shower now. You better leave me some of the coffee," she warned him before walking out of the kitchen, still fighting the urge to smile. He raised his empty spoon in a salute as he chewed.

Safely in the bathroom, Sasha locked the door and leaned against it, taking a few deep breaths to calm herself down. Her skin heated and her nerves jittered. And she was a little light-headed.

Yes, there was some awkwardness. But they were still Fox and Sasha. They would be okay.

With a sigh, she pushed away from the door and crossed to the shower, turning the water on. Now was not the time to be disappointed that he hadn't joined her. No, she'd meant what she said about being adults. They couldn't let what happened distract either of them. Except, she still wanted him.

***

It was a relief to Fox when he arrived at the team's press conference, and discovered that most of the attention was focused on Henri and the exiting goalie. He mostly just sat off to the side, presumably out of frame for most of the broadcasts. There were only three questions that came his way, and they were mostly about his family.

"How do your parents feel about your big break?" one reporter asked. "It must have been intimidating, when you

told them that, of all things, you wanted to play hockey."
There was a murmur of laughter from the crowd, and even
Fox smiled.

"Bryce helped me out with breaking the news on that
one," he joked. "He'd already had to go through it when he
told them he wanted to play tennis, so... I think they were
surprised. But they've always been pretty great about making
sure we all had the opportunities to explore our interests and
talents, whatever they have been."

Another reporter jumped in. "As the first Coulter to
branch out into hockey, do you feel like there's as much
pressure on you to perform to your family's high standards, or
is it easier not having a specific relative to compare yourself to
in that regard?"

"I don't know that I have anything I can compare it to,
to be honest," Fox said with a shrug. "Dax and Echo have both
gone down that road where my grandfather's concerned, but
I'm not either of them, so I can't say I know what it was like
for them with any certainty. I only know what it's been like for
me."

"And how would you describe that?" the reporter
hastily followed up.

"It's been... I'm definitely hard on myself. But we all
have a tendency to be hard on ourselves, and maybe that's
what pushes us to do the best we can. All I know is I've always
loved hockey, and I'm really excited for the opportunity I'm
being given," he finished, getting himself back on track and
looking to Coach Tremblay. Coach didn't look too irritated
and took back his command of the press in the room.

After it was over, Fox tried to apologize to Coach
about his little tangent, but Tremblay cut him off and assured
him he'd done fine, and that he'd see him suited up on the

bench for the game in a few hours.

Fox found some time between the end of the press conference and the time he would need to suit up for the game to call his parents and check in.

"I know that I got a little off-track there," he started off. He'd never been as savvy as Echo or Bryce when it came to handling the media. Nor had he been the focus of its spotlight before, either. Dax had been, and probably still was. The most prominent of the siblings when it came to the media and instantaneous recognition, but since he and Asha had become a couple, he'd become a master of handling reporters and the press. Even Gage seemed to be more natural, when it came to answering questions about himself.

"You did fine," his father said, interrupting Fox's rambling. "You expressed yourself. And you're probably right about us Coulters in general. We do have a tendency to be hard on ourselves," he admitted with a little laugh.

"I'll work on it before my next press conference, which hopefully won't be for a while," Fox added. "I'm sitting on the bench tonight, and that's where it sounds like I'll be most nights, so it probably *will* be a while."

"For the team, maybe," his father said somberly.

"As opposed to…?"

"Your mother and I have been talking with my doctors, and…I'm going to have to step down from the company. At least, take on a less-demanding role for a while," he said. "I have to figure things out with the lawyers, and there'll be more than a few meetings to decide who'll take over for me as president…but we're going to have to make a public announcement sometime soon."

Fox swallowed before asking, "How soon?"

"A couple of weeks. Not long."

"Dad, I know everything is crazy, and you need time off to get healthy. Do you want me to maybe, try and fill in for a bit? I'm not Bryce, or Echo — hell, or even Dax — but I could study up quick."

His father exhaled softly, and Fox could hear the slight smile in his voice. Instead of saying "Yes, I could use the help," his father said, "Thank you, Fox. But I'm not going to ask you to do that. You have to focus on hockey. That's always been the most important thing to you. Your mother is actually going to step in to my slot for a while. She's going to hand off the charity work to your grandmother, and fill in for me. She's extremely adept."

As his father spoke, Fox couldn't explain why the hole in his chest only seemed to widen. Yes, it was true, he had absolutely zero interest in working at Legacy Sports. It wasn't his dream. He wasn't even sure that he was smart enough to do it. But like his siblings before him, he at least wanted to be asked. He wanted his parents to believe in him. Right now, it looked as if they didn't. To his family, he was just Fox. Affable, but not one that they would trust with the legacy of the family. The legacy of the Coulter name. It stung almost as badly as knowing he was only called up to the Brawlers as a second choice.

Although it hurt, there was no way he was going to show his father that. The old man had enough to worry about without tending to Fox's ego, too. This wasn't about ego. All Fox wanted was to be considered capable of stepping up when it was needed. Right now, he was almost worse than the black sheep—he was poor old Fox.

He forced a smile, though. "Okay. Well, I know you have Bryce and Echo to call on, but if you did need me, I could do it."

There was a long pause. "Son, we know you could."

Fox wasn't certain, but that sounded like a note of dishonesty in his father's voice. He cleared his throat. "Well, uh…give me a heads-up when you know for sure, okay?" he requested.

"Don't worry. I'll be calling all of you kids before it goes public."

"Thanks, Dad. Love you."

"Love you too, son. And congratulations. You'll do great. One of your first home games, your mother and I will be there. Promise."

Chapter Ten

Two whole weeks went by without a fuckup from Fox. Not that he wasn't trying for one. He was on the bench, so he couldn't screw up. And as for Sasha, he'd managed to keep his hands off her. At least in reality. And that shit wasn't easy. Especially with her running around looking hot and sexy. And fuckable. Every time she laughed, he was desperate to touch her. But every night in his dreams, man oh man, did he touch her. He touched her in *all kinds* of ways. Ways she'd hinted about with the brunette.

When his father finally made his announcement, Fox felt weird about not telling Sasha. He told her everything. Or, he used to…before they'd screwed like mad in her kitchen. It was only about two weeks later that his father announced his illness to the world. They'd kept their discussions focused on work, her big semester project, and how he was adjusting to the new team. Never to that night, and not once about his father.

When he asked about her story, though, she would vaguely say that it was coming together and she was pleased, and then she'd turn the conversation to Fox and how things were going with the team. "Is it weird with your friends, still?"

she asked.

He shrugged. "A little. They were extra-hard on me during a scrimmage this week. But I was able to keep their shots from going in."

She nodded, even as she frowned. "I'm sorry shit is so weird because of me."

"Hey," he said, putting a hand on her knee then immediately withdrawing it. "You didn't fuck up. Besides, things got a little better after that," he had added with a shrug.

"Well, I'm still sorry I have to miss the first game. I didn't make you a sign."

"I know, it's cool." A part of him was relieved it would be an away game, and that he wouldn't have the extra pressure of his family coming to see him. Sasha, though, he would have liked to have there.

"It's not something I need right now, and it isn't something they need right now," he'd said.

She was quiet for a moment. "Why didn't you tell me about your dad? Is there anything I can do?"

Fox shook his head. "No. It'll be okay. He just has to rest."

She frowned. "Okay. But you know if you want to talk, I'm here, right?"

Heat prickled under his skin. He didn't want

to talk. "Yeah, I hear you. I promise, if I ever want to talk, you're my gal."

***

Fox might not feel like talking, but that didn't mean Sasha didn't worry. "How long has he been sick?" Sasha asked Echo at her next fitting.

"A while. My parents told me but wanted to keep it quiet as long as possible. They didn't even tell the boys for…months," Echo explained as she sorted through her fabric samples.

Sasha was wearing the prototype runner's outfit Echo had designed, but after having learned more about the fabric manufacturer's dyeing processes, she was worried the material wouldn't wear well.

"So you don't think it…*means* anything that Fox didn't give me a heads-up?" Sasha asked. "I mean…he's my best friend *and* my roommate. If something like this was bothering him…I want to make sure he knows he can trust me with it."

Echo frowned at Sasha. "Of course, he knows that. I don't think he talks to anyone the way he talks to you, to be honest. If he didn't tell you…my guess is he hasn't sorted it out, himself."

Sasha got that in a way. "But to let me find out the way I did? The guys in sports were going through the interview footage, and they pulled me

in because they know I know your family. It was…"
Sasha sighed. "It was surprising and…scary, I
guess. Our families have always been pretty close,
and it was just unexpected."

"It's not as serious as the media are making it
out to be," Echo tried to reassure her. "He's
undergoing treatment, and he's actually doing a bit
better—feeling better, that is. It's not something that
can be cured. The main reason they had to finally go
public with it is because he has to step down from
the company for a while. The treatments take a toll.
It was a business move more than anything."

Sasha let the issue drop, standing still to
allow Echo to move about her and make her
decision, while Sasha tried to figure out why Fox's
silence on the issue bothered her so much. It hurt.
But it wasn't a personal hurt. She felt hurt on his
behalf. It had to be difficult finally tackling the big
leagues while things were so difficult personally.
She hated the idea that he was hurting over
something and she was too oblivious to notice, or he
felt too weirded out to talk to her. Sleeping with
him had changed everything.

To her surprise, he was already at the
apartment when she returned from work.

"Hey Sash," he said in greeting as he sorted
through his duffel bags in the living room.

"You're back. How'd your first game go? I mean, I *did* watch it so I know you did great. But how are *you* feeling about it? Were you nervous?"

He chuckled. "A little distracted, yeah. But good. I just didn't realize the announcement was going to be made when it was. So I had to field questions."

Sasha put her purse and keys down and headed over to where he'd been crouched on the floor, and knelt beside him. It was an awkward feat in her pencil skirt, but she managed. Reaching out to slip an arm around him and rest her head on his shoulder, she said, "I was just worried about you. *Are* you okay? It must be a pretty tough thing to have to deal with. Especially as you already have all this pressure."

Fox shrugged. "I've known he was sick for a while now. But he didn't want people to know until he was ready, and…"

"It wasn't your secret to tell," Sasha finished for him. "I get it."

"It was worse when he and Mom first told us. Well, when Echo let it slip and they had to admit to what was really going on," Fox corrected himself. "His doctors were still trying to figure out what was wrong with him, so that was pretty scary. The not knowing. It was easier once they said it was an autoimmune thing, though. I'm still not completely sure *what* that means, I just know it isn't cancer. Anyway, once it had a name and they could give him stuff to treat some of his symptoms, it got easier."

"If there is *anything* I can do for you, you know you just have to ask and I'll do it. And if you want to move back in with your parents—"

"Whoa, now," Fox's brows drew up. "It's not that serious. And there isn't really anything I can do to help one way or another—"

"I'm sorry. I just...I know you moved in here as kind of a favor to me, and I wasn't sure if maybe you felt obligated or something to stay, but since I've started working with Echo, money isn't as tight as it was, so—"

He put his hands up. "You needing financial help was the excuse for me to move in here with you. I'd have done it anyway, if you'd asked. I love living with you," he assured her.

Something tingled low in her belly. Okay, maybe a little lower than her belly.

Sasha sighed with relief. "And I love living with you. Now, if you don't really need cheering up over what's going on with your dad, do you want to celebrate your first official NHL game? You were pretty impressive. A four-to-two win for the team, never relinquishing the lead, and those two goals were totally not your fault. I mean, those two guys on your team should *not* have both been penalized, and if it had only been five on four during the power play instead of five on three, that goal never would have gotten in. And pulling the goalie during the last minute of the game? I mean, I know everyone does it but they weren't going to make up the three-goal difference."

Fox laughed. "Well, I'm still not happy about them. The one at the last minute, especially. But thanks. It was a bit nerve-wracking. I still think it'll be worse for my first home game in net, but we're in an every-other-day pattern for a while, so it could be another week before I get in there again."

"I still say we should celebrate," Sasha insisted, carefully using Fox's shoulder to brace herself as she struggled to rise.

"After what happened last time, you really want to go out to a bar with me again?" Fox joked but then stammered. "Not that—"

"I know what you meant," Sasha cut him off. She didn't need him knowing she *didn't* mind the idea of things ending that way a second time. "Actually a few friends of mine from college are having a little party of their own. Want to try that? We might find you that girl you're looking for."

His eyes narrowed a little, and he said, "So…a college party?"

"So you'll come? I don't know how crazy it'll be. If it's crazy at all."

"Fine," Fox nodded slowly. "Take me to your college party. Show me your academic ways."

"Hop in the shower and put on something casual. You smell like a locker room. I'm going to go figure out what to wear."

***

The party was in the early stages when they arrived. He couldn't explain it, but he immediately felt out of place. He was happy he'd tossed on jeans and a T-shirt with just a funky blazer over it, instead of the button-down he'd planned on. Sasha was wearing a see-through shirt, so that the dark outlines of her bra were clearly visible. It wasn't the lacy one he was so intimately familiar with, but damned if he didn't want to be. She'd paired it with a sassy, floating skirt. The moment he caught sight of her long expanse of leg, he wanted to spread them wide open and bury his face in her heat. Licking her until she screamed. He was so caught up in his fantasy that he missed what she said. "Huh?"

Sasha frowned at him and rolled her eyes. "Relax. You'll be fine," she assured him. "You've been to a million parties."

She was right. And this wasn't his first college party. But he couldn't shake the feeling that they were on a date. After introductions were made they found the keg, and his mood vastly improved. All it took was one frat-boy wannabe trying to perform a handstand on a keg and failing miserably for Fox to decide it was worth attending.

"Let's grab something to drink and walk around a bit," Sasha suggested, clearly pleased that he seemed to be enjoying himself. "I need to find the rest of my friends and introduce you."

Her friends were grouped in the living room, chattering loudly and laughing raucously. Sasha and Fox sat at the outskirts, listening raptly and doing their best to fade into the background so as to not draw too much attention to themselves. But that didn't last long.

"I thought you said you were bringing your boyfriend?" one of her friends whispered loudly to Sasha. She flushed and explained just as loudly that, no, she had broken up with Ryan more than a six weeks ago.

"I said I was bringing my *roommate*," she clarified.

"But you live with your boyfriend," the friend insisted. Everyone laughed at the extent to which the poor girl was intoxicated, and when she heard everyone else laughing, the drunk friend laughed, too.

"I *was* living with my boyfriend until I broke up with him and I kicked him out," she explained again.

"Don't bother," another friend chimed in while mixing a few types of juice with vodka and sipping the mixture until she nodded in approval. "She won't remember what you tell her anyway, and I don't think any of us care."

"Gee, thanks guys," she said, taking a sip of her own rum and Coke.

"Let's play 'Never Have I Ever,'" the deeply inebriated friend suggested.

"How do you play that?" Fox asked to a round of giggles that made him feel a little ridiculous.

"Don't worry, not-boyfriend," the drunk one said, jovially elbowing Fox in the side. "We'll teach ya."

And teach they did. Over the course of the next hour, he learned all sorts of things about Sasha. Sexual things. Things that would drive him crazy later.

For example, she'd never had sex in public. She'd never been tied up. She'd never had anal sex. At the rate they were going, he'd be wasted in no time.

The rules were to drink if you had done whatever was called out. And Fox had done…a lot. Turns out, he was a very bad boy.

When one of her friends announced she'd never had sex in a car, he gawked when Sasha didn't drink. "You're joking?"

She shook her head. "Nope."

Before he could stop himself, he said, "We are going to remedy that at the earliest possible convenience."

Chapter Eleven

Holy shit, Fox was so sexy. His voice, low and hushed so only she would hear, sent shivers through her body. Did he plan on them remedying that problem tonight? Because she was game. *No, dumbass, he's teasing.* She'd had to excuse herself so she could splash water on her face. "Behave."

"I'll try."

When she returned, Fox was missing, along with Nell.

"Hey Erica, where did Fox go?"

"Don't look at me," Erica said with a shrug. "She whispered something to him, and he helped her get up and they went that way." Erica pointed toward the stairs leading up to the bedrooms.

An unexpected stab of jealousy and disgust pierced her heart. *But I don't want him. Liar.* Damn, that hurt. She and Fox weren't together, a point she'd been emphasizing for weeks. There were times when she thought that being with him was something she might want, but she was so damn scared. She needed their friendship.

After that memorable night, she'd been less afraid of sex messing with their dynamic, but there was still so much that could go wrong.

Fire burned in her belly. He wasn't hers. She

had no right, and she knew it.

She turned the corner at the landing and spotted Fox quietly closing a door behind him and turning to come back down the stairs. He was alone and looked startled, but a wide smile spread over his face. Sasha jogged up the stairs to join him.

"You wandered off," she said gently.

"I didn't 'wander' anywhere. Your friend leaned in and made me a proposal that she probably thought sounded interesting."

"You didn't take her up on it?"

He frowned and stared down at her. "I told her to lead the way, and when we got to her bedroom I put her to bed. Tucked her in and everything, even found her little trash bin and put it on the bed beside her so she won't have to look for it later. And she *will* need it. Hopefully, she can sleep it off."

Relief flooded Sasha, quickly followed by guilt. He didn't have to justify himself to her. She was ruining this. Why couldn't she be normal?

"Thanks for taking care of her," Sasha told him. "Sorry about…" She shrugged, unable to put everything into words. Uncertain how he'd react if she tried.

"No problem. Besides, I came with you." He shoved his hands in his pockets.

She reached down and took one hand out. "Come on," she said leading him down the hall, glancing at the rooms on either side until she spotted one with an open door. Melissa's name was plastered across the front. Sasha was pretty sure she'd spotted Melissa cheering her boyfriend and his friends on in a game of beer pong set up on the dining room table, so it would be some time before they came up looking to use the bedroom.

She ushered Fox through the door and closed it behind them, instinctively turning the lock. "There you go," she said with a flourish. "Peace and quiet."

Fox flipped the light on and looked around the room. It was pretty small—Melissa had forced a queen-sized bed into a room that was only meant for a twin, leaving little space to move around. She wasn't one to keep things neat and tidy, either. Her dirty clothes littered the floor, and were interspersed with textbooks and notebooks for her various classes.

"Is this what it looks like in dorms?" Fox inquired, pointing to one of Melissa's bras hanging by its straps on a bedpost.

"Actually..." She looked around at the posters, decorative lights, and multitude of mirrors. "Yeah. I've seen my share of dorms that look *just* like this."

Fox laughed and plopped down on the bed, leaning back on his elbows for a moment before laying all the way back. "God. I didn't realize how exhausted I was until now. Though some of it might be the beer."

She lay down beside him, both of them stretched sideways on the bed with their legs hanging off. They both stared at the ceiling, the only surface of the room Melissa hadn't gotten around to decorating. Their shoulders touched, their arms running alongside each other down to the backs of their hands.

"I'm sorry about your dad being sick," she whispered.

"Me too." Fox's voice was quiet and thick.

"Do…do you think that, him being sick, you being worried about him, do you think that was part of why you didn't make the team during the tryouts? Was it too distracting?"

The bed moved as Fox sighed deeply.

"No," he finally answered. "I think I wanted it too much, and I have a nasty habit of sabotaging myself."

She propped herself up on an elbow. "You do not sabotage yourself."

"Come on," Fox challenged. "I choke *all the*

time. I can take care of what I need to do until the pressure gets turned up, and then…" He raised his hands to his throat and made wheezing noises until Sasha elbowed him gently with a laugh.

"Well, you didn't choke during the game the other night," she reminded him.

"What do you call letting a goal in during the last minute of the game?"

"Nerves. I think you get in your head and can be too hard on yourself."

"How is that different from self-sabotage, exactly?"

"Because with self-sabotage there's an element of thinking. Particularly that on some level, probably subconsciously, you don't deserve what you're trying to get…or you're unaware that you don't *really* want it." She propped herself up on her elbow so she could look down at him. "But I know you. You *do* want this. *And* you deserve it. You know you do. So, you've just got a bad case of nerves to work out."

"I do want it," he admitted after a minute. He raised his hand enough to run his fingers along her forearm. "And I'm not just talking about hockey. I think my self-sabotage goes beyond that."

Sasha shifted on the bed so that she was on her side, facing him, and could throw her arm across him and rest her head on his shoulder in a sort of hug.

"There you go being too hard on yourself again. You'll get it. You'll adjust and be fine," she assured him, then raised her head enough to give him a comforting peck on the cheek before resting against him again and closing her eyes.

He slid his right arm over to clasp her left hand where it rested against his chest, stroking the back of her hand with his, twining his fingers with hers. Sasha snuggled closer against him so his left arm could circle her back instead of being crushed between them. In the process, he pressed her body against his. Something shifted between them, and when she reopened her eyes, she found him watching her intently, leaning closer.

"What are we doing?" she asked softly.

"I'm going to take care of a few things on your 'Never Have I Ever' list," he told her as he eased her legs open and crouched at the side of the bed. She started to sit up, but he upset her balance when he slid his hands under her thighs and wrapped his arms around them, leaving her completely open to him.

"Fox?" She panted in anticipation as he rubbed his cheek against the tender skin of her inner thigh.

He'd shaved sometime in the morning, so while there was no scratchy stubble, there was still a distinct friction. "There were a few things you didn't drink to that everyone should have to drink to," he murmured against her thigh.

She didn't have to ask him which of her responses he intended to rectify. Her fingers dug into the bedspread as Fox's tongue went to work on the sensitive skin of her thighs. Then, with his thumb, he eased back the elastic of her panty. "Fuck, you're wet." He settled her legs so they were hooked over his shoulders, while he ran his right hand from her knee up over her hip to her navel. The muscles in her belly contracted violently, as she fought to direct the course of his tongue by wriggling her hips. When he sucked on her, she dug her heels into his back, arching and crying out as she shook in ecstasy.

She was still trembling when the warmth of his head between her legs disappeared, and he reappeared hovering above her, grinning. She managed a weak smile in return as he dropped his lips to hers for a kiss, his tongue finding hers so that she could taste herself.

There was warm pressure along her left side where he was gently grinding his erection against her hip, the bulge impossible to ignore. She tried to loop her leg around him to show she was ready for him to enter her, but she couldn't get her leg to follow her direction. She couldn't get any of her limbs to respond just yet.

"So that's one," Fox teased, pressing kisses along her jaw and playfully biting her earlobe.

"You…had more…in mind?" Sasha managed to say.

Fox rose to a kneeling position so he could unfasten the belt below Sasha's breasts. "Every woman deserves multiple orgasms. And the other night doesn't count. We slept in between, so I'm going to fix that."

"Fox—"

"I have another road trip coming up next week. East coast, this time, so I'll be gone a few days." He slipped the belt from around her waist and dropped it onto the floor, then unsnapped Sasha's blouse. "I was thinking it would be nice to have a few keepsakes that I can look at to keep me from getting too lonely." He kissed the valley between her breasts, but Sasha slid her hands in his hair and then tipped his head back so she could meet his eye.

"You want to take pictures of me? You first. Wouldn't porn do the trick?"

Fox put a gentle hand over her mouth to get

her attention. She bit at the palm of his hand playfully, remembering that it was Fox she was dealing with, and not Ryan.

"You want to know why I want pictures of you, specifically?"

His hand was still over her mouth as she nodded but he removed it to take her hand and gently lift it off her blouse so he could push the fabric aside. "You might not think so, but I could pick your breasts out of a lineup," he told her. Her skeptical expression made him laugh. "It's true," he insisted. His fingers skimmed the edge of one cup of her bra raising goose pimples on her skin.

"You've only seen them once. Not enough times to be able to do that," she challenged.

He tugged aside the fabric. "You've got a little freckle right here." He bent his head and kissed the spot. His tongue flashed out, making her breath hitch and her nipple tighten. "And there's a scar just over here above the right one." He kissed that mark, too.

"Chicken pox," Sasha whispered.

Fox grinned as he exposed the appendectomy scar, then kissed that mark, as well.

He raised himself above her again, his weight on his forearms. "I want pictures of *you* because I know your body." His voice was low and husky as his lips skimmed her collarbone, pausing over the spot where she'd broken it skating with him on the rink his parents set up behind their house when the two of them were nine. "I've fallen asleep on your breasts," he reminded her. "I know exactly how far around me your arms stretch. I don't want just anyone. I want *you*. The question is, do you want me?"

Sasha smiled as she released a long exhale, her hands tangling in his hair to bring him down for a lingering kiss.

"Okay," she agreed. "But you have to pay for every photo you take. If you get to look at me, I want to look at you, too. Each shot will cost you an article of clothing."

He laughed and began removing the jacket he'd worn, remembering to reach into the pocket to pull out his cell phone before letting it drop to the floor.

Sasha took a deep breath, flushing as she undid the rest of the buttons on her blouse. When she slipped her arms out of her bra, Fox licked his lips, watching her hungrily. She lay back on the bed and raised her arms over her head, shielding her eyes from the first flash.

With each piece of clothing he dropped, each flash of the camera, Sasha grew more comfortable, more playful. She posed more carefully, imitating old pin-up girl poses for a few shots, then moving on to her interpretations of some other iconic nude photo shoots she recalled. She posed with her hands over her breasts, helping push them up, arching her back with her knees drawn up and to the side so he could get a shot of her ass, and lying on her stomach with her feet in the air and her hair draped across her back.

As he dropped his boxers and stepped out of them, he moved toward the bed where Sasha was once again on her back. She was still damp between her legs from before, but the sight of him approaching her with his dick erect sent a flood of warmth through her body that settled low in her belly.

"Yes," she said, opening her legs to him. "Please."

"Last one," he said, raising the phone, as the tip of his cock slid down her folds, parting her lips and pressing against her center.

Sasha threw her head back, closed her eyes, and stopped listening. All of her being was focused on the sensation as he pushed home, sliding with an easy steadiness that built the heat in her belly. There was a faint thud as he tossed the phone onto the bed beside her, and then his hands glided up and down her legs, catching under one knee, pressing it higher so he could deepen his thrusts.

Sasha raised her other leg into a similar position, and he grabbed hold of it, Fox's hips occasionally jutting into the backs of her thighs as he increased his pace.

She drew her legs higher, panting for him to go faster and harder as he pounded, only losing her grip on her legs when she lost her grip on herself and her release shuddered through her. But Fox wasn't done with her. He buried his face in her neck, tugged her hair so she was forced to arch back. His cock hit that sensitive spot inside over and over again, until she cried out once more. It was only then that Fox came deep inside her, his body shuddering on top of her, his head coming to rest in the valley between her breasts. His panting breath chilled her left nipple and caused her own breath to hitch before he lifted his mouth in search of hers and kissed her deeply.

***

"Jesus, Sash, you're going to kill me."

She couldn't help but laugh. "Yeah, but what a way to go, right?"

He pulled her with him and rolled them to their sides before giving her a gentle peck. "What are we doing here, Sash? Because right now, I know it's been torture *not* to touch you."

She swallowed hard. "I don't know. This was supposed to be fun and easy. But now it's intense and complicated."

He was silent for a beat. "I know this was supposed to be a *friends with benefits* thing, but clearly, after what we just did, we're not going to keep pretending this only happens once in a while. I want this to happen more than that. Everyday, twice a day. If I could stay inside you forever, I would."

Sasha ducked her head. "Fox, I know how you get. You hit them and quit them. We're friends. We don't need this to be complicated."

He kissed the end of her nose. "It's not complicated. You just don't know you belong in my bed yet." He shrugged. "It's okay. I plan to keep reminding you until you realize I'm for real. I don't want to be the interim guy. Rebound guy."

She tipped her head up to meet his gaze. "You're not. I'm the one who's interim. I know that."

He stared at her for a long moment. Then the kiss he gave her was achingly soft and sweet. "You go to sleep for a few. When you wake up, I'll show you again that you're not interim to me. And I'll just keep reminding you until you get it."

Sasha didn't think she'd be able to sleep, but after three Fox-assisted orgasms, she was ready to collapse. And when she woke up, he did show her again.

***

Eventually, the real world intruded, and the sounds of the party started to diminish. They needed to go home.

Getting back into their clothes was less fun, but having crossed that line between friendship and physical intimacy again, she understood that Fox was right. They'd be doing this again. And again, and...well, she got the picture. The only question was how long before he got bored.

As Sasha located her discarded bra and slipped her arms back through the straps, Fox came up behind her to help re-clasp it, his fingers brushing across her shoulder blades in the process.

Sasha was in trouble. This was Fox. She loved everything about him. Always had. But she was going to get hurt. And there was no protecting her heart. Not from the boy she'd adored since she was six, and certainly not from the man he was now.

"Oh, whoops," Fox said, as he put his jacket back on and reached for their phones on the nightstand. "I think I took those pictures on *your* phone instead of mine," he told her.

Sasha finished adjusting the belt that held her skirt in place. It was a bit more wrinkled than it had been when they arrived at the party, and her blouse was looking a bit disheveled too. "Yup, that *is* my phone."

"Here," Fox said, "I'll just send them to myself and delete them off here for you."

"What? Don't delete them," she objected then blushed under his amused gaze. "I—I can delete them myself when I'm ready."

He grinned as he finished typing his email address into her phone and hit the send button. He whispered in her ear as he slipped the phone back into her hand. "Next time, I can be the subject and we can see how you do as photographer." He pressed a kiss to the corner of her smile, but she turned to give him a real kiss before he could pull away again, his words sending a quiet thrill through her body—*Next time.*

Chapter Twelve

The morning after the party, Sasha woke to find several messages in her inbox. All of them had to do with the copy of the story she'd submitted for feedback. Her professor had loved it and had a few very minor notes for her to incorporate before submitting it for her final grade. It was encouraging, so maybe she'd gotten away with not using Fox.

After reading the next email, she realized she wasn't so lucky. Her bosses at the station had taken a look at the story and were so pleased with it they wanted to run it, but with an edit. They were adding in Fox. And because of a problem with one of their other human-interest pieces, they wanted to run it *today*. She sat up in bed, the panic settling in.

It would play first during their midday coverage, having been teased during the early-morning local coverage, and would be available on their website for streaming after that. Plus, they were going to run it during each of the evening news cycles as well. They were hoping to get her to fill in more information for a bio on the website to go with her byline.

She jumped out of bed and ran to Fox's room to see if he was still there. She still had a small chance of being able to tell him first. But he'd already left for practice. She frantically tried to call Ida to see if she would hold off on airing it until she could finish it properly with the help of her professor's notes and suggestions. And to give her time to warn Fox. When Ida answered, Sasha breathed a sigh of relief.

"Oh my God, thank God I reached you, Ida."

She could hear the smile in her mentor's voice. "If it isn't our intrepid reporter. How does it feel to have your first big story out?"

"That's why I'm calling. We can't do this. It's going to hurt Fox when he sees it. I didn't think you were going to push the story out yet. It was never my intention to have him be front and center in the story."

There was a long pause. "Look, I know you two have some kind of relationship, but let me be clear. You are an intern. You do not get to dictate what we do and do not air. We own your time and your work." Ida's voice softened. "Look, it really is a fantastic development for your career. Try and enjoy it."

She hung up with Ida and ran her hands through her hair. To have the station air her piece even before she had completed her internship, before the assignment was technically due or finished, was a huge thing. Sasha prayed that Fox would understand, or at least forgive her, when he found out. She didn't bother trying to convince herself that Fox wouldn't realize he was the inspiration behind the piece. Especially now that they were editing it to include some footage of him. Fox wasn't stupid.

He wouldn't answer his cell phone during his practice, and she had no way to know for sure when he was done for the day. So unless she wanted to tell him in a voicemail and have her explanation recorded so that it could haunt her forever, she would just have to wait until later in the day to call him, or wait for him to call her. As soon as he heard about it and saw the story for himself, he would call.

She had her last fittings with Echo that morning, and there would be some photography involved, as well, in preparation for the formal photo shoot coming up.

Sasha arrived at Echo's studio almost forty minutes early to find it locked. She sank to the floor in front of the door with her coffee in hand and started perusing the station's website for references to her story. She was supposed to be excited about getting her story on air. She was supposed to be calling her friends to gush about it or her father to gloat about her success. And she *wanted* to be excited, but the person she could always count on to get excited about things like this was Fox.

By the time Echo arrived with Jen forty-five minutes later, the beginning of the midday news cycle had started, and the station had posted the video of the story to their website. Sasha had watched it on mute five times. Objectively, she was proud of how the piece itself had turned out. The interviews flowed well together, and she had plenty of research to back it up. She'd have to remember to send the list of linked sources to her boss so they could post it on the website for anyone interested. She'd watched and listened to herself many times in the process of editing the story together, but it was still surreal to watch it on her phone through the station's site.

"What're you watching?" Echo said as she moved to unlock the door to her studio.

Sasha sighed. Maybe Echo and Jen would be able to help her figure out how to deal with the blowback from Fox. "The station decided to run my piece. The one I was doing for the final project of my internship," she told them as she pushed herself up from the floor.

"That's fantastic!" Echo and Jen exclaimed,

displaying the excitement Sasha wished she could muster.

"It is. It's a huge deal for my prospects with the station after I graduate, and with other networks if I have to look elsewhere," Sasha agreed, following them into the now-familiar studio.

"Are you hungover from celebrating, or something?" Jen asked. "'Cause you don't sound all that enthusiastic about it."

"Watch it. I bet you guys can guess why I'm a little unenthused," she told them, trailing off as she handed over the phone and turned the sound back on. She wandered off while they watched it, not needing to look at it personally to know every single word and frame.

"That was wonderful," Jen assured Sasha after it wrapped up. "The depth you were able to achieve in that amount of time…the interviews…"

Sasha looked to Echo, who was watching her with sympathy. "You're worried about Fox, aren't you," she stated, rather than asked.

Sasha nodded. "It—he *inspired* it, but not in the way that I'm afraid he'll take it. And they used footage of some of his earlier games. It's just, for years, I've listened to him every time he gets his hopes up over an opportunity, only to fall at the last minute, and the way that he blames himself every time. And I *know* he gets into his head sometimes and panics so that he freezes, and every time it happens he gets worse the next time around. And that doesn't mean that I don't think he can do it and make it as far as he wants to. I *know* that he can, and this piece... I don't know, maybe I was trying to see if there was some way that looking into it from this angle could help me understand *how* to help him snap out of whatever it is he does to himself that makes him choke all the time." Sasha rambled, all of the fears and rationalization of working on the story for the last few weeks tumbling from her mind in a jumble.

"He'll get over it," Echo assured her.

Sasha wasn't so sure. "It's a betrayal. *I* betrayed him," she insisted. "He's not going to let that go. Nor should he."

"Oh, no, he won't let it go, but that doesn't mean he won't get over it. He's still riding you on mistakes you made when you were in grade school," Echo reminded her. "And *you* still give him a hard time about the stupid things he's done over the years. It's part of how you guys are as friends."

Sasha flushed and slid her glance away from Echo.

"Or is there more going on between you now?" Echo asked slowly.

"Are you two *together*?" Jen pressed.

"I—I don't know," Sasha admitted. "Things *are* changing between us, and they seem to be moving in that direction. But I wanted to tell him about the story, first. I wanted to tell him before anything happened between us because he's my friend. But I just haven't been able to figure out *how* to tell him."

"Wait," Jen interjected and leaned in closer, speaking quietly though there was no one else in the room. "What do you mean, *before anything happened*? You *slept* with Fox?"

Sasha didn't respond, but Jen's and Echo's expressions recognized the confirmation in her silence.

"It all just sort of happened." The story spilled out. "And now I feel like a horrible person for this mess, and I just don't know what to do that could make it right."

"First off, call him and talk to him about it. There's a chance he hasn't seen it yet, and if you can be the one to tell him, go for it," Echo advised.

"And if you're sleeping with him, then—" Jen started, but Echo interrupted.

"Don't finish that thought. At least, not when I'm around." Echo made a choking noise. "Just like he doesn't want to hear about me and Cole, I don't want the details. He's my little brother and I know that he — you know. But it doesn't mean I want to talk about. Anyway, Sasha, this is between you and Fox, so you're going to have to talk to him about it. But you guys are friends, even if you are moving in *that* direction, and you guys will be fine."

Echo's confidence in their relationship, whatever form it might be taking, took the edge off Sasha's fears. "Okay. I'll call him now," she said, pulling her phone out. "Unless you were ready to get started…" She trailed off, looking to the racks of clothes and the smattering of mannequins in the studio's lofty space.

"Call him," Echo insisted. "We just got here and need to settle in. You'll have plenty of time to sort things out with Fox."

Before Sasha could even start dialing her phone rang, and according to the caller ID, it was Fox.

"Speak of the devil," she muttered, before taking a deep breath and answering.

Chapter Thirteen

Fox spent much of the next day at morning practice reliving every moment of that party. He'd been tempted to follow her into her bedroom, or invite her into his own when they'd gone home. But he didn't want her to think he only wanted sex from her, and he wanted to give her time to adjust to what he'd said. This wasn't temporary for him.

Each time he heard the smack of a stick on a puck and the resultant thunk as he deflected it off his stick or pads, he heard the cheesy sound her phone had made as he'd snapped those sexy pictures of her. Those pics would remain forever emblazoned in his mind. Particularly the last little video he'd shot before his hand had started shaking with the need to grab hold of her while he pushed his cock deeper.

He hadn't brought himself to flip through them yet. They were still prominent enough in his mind's eye that he didn't require the potent reality of the images themselves to get off. And he hadn't had the time or privacy necessary for when he did start looking through them.

It took Fox a few moments to realize that the shots had stopped coming at him. The ice around him was littered with pucks. But when he noticed the awe with which his teammates were standing around watching him, he grew self-conscious and looked for Coach Tremblay. He found the man grinning and clutching his clipboard to his chest. With a brief motion, Tremblay signaled to an assistant to start gathering up the discarded pucks while he started making notations.

Fox grew uncomfortable as he skated slightly out of the crease, corralling the loose pucks into a group to make it easier for the assistant to collect them.

"Great job, man," the guy said with a clap to Fox's well-padded shoulder. "I've never seen anything like it."

Fox shrugged in response, unsure what was so impressive about his performance. He turned to retrieve the pucks that had made it into the net only to see there weren't any. He'd stopped every shot that came his way without even realizing it. No wonder everyone was quiet. *He* was floored, and he tried to think back to figure out how he'd managed to do it. But all thoughts of Sasha were all that were in his head.

He knew she wasn't looking for a relationship, and he wasn't entirely convinced that what had passed between them wasn't just her rebounding from Ryan. He knew that *he* wanted something more with her, but what exactly that something was, he wasn't sure. He knew he wanted her. And he also knew he didn't want anyone else with their hands on her, either.

Things were just so easy with Sasha. He didn't second-guess himself with her the way he did with everything else in his life. At the same time, he didn't feel like they had to make any decisions right away. There was no pressure. He wasn't seeing anyone, and to the best of his knowledge, she wasn't seeing anyone else either.

"Hold on, Coulter," Coach Tremblay said before Fox could follow his teammates down to the locker room to wash up and head out for the day.

"Yeah, Coach?" Fox asked, tucking his helmet tighter under his arm.

"Listen, Coulter, Henri's been fighting off a cold the last week. You going in net the other day gave him a good rest, but he still hasn't been able to shake it. He's willing to play through it as best he can, but after how you did today, I'm thinking I might bench him tomorrow and see if we can't get him a bit more rest to get rid of this thing once and for all."

"You want me to start? Tomorrow?" Fox wasn't sure he'd heard correctly.

"You've been doing well in the practices, and

you held your own the other night," Coach Tremblay nodded. "We're not going up against the Rajun Cajuns, so it won't be as high-pressured as some of the other games coming up on our schedule. I think you're ready. What do you say? How do you think you've been doing?"

Fox fought to control his expression, but could tell from the amusement evident in Coach Tremblay's that he was failing miserably. "I guess, I don't know. I was just...in the zone earlier, but... Yeah, sure. I have to have my first home game sometime, right? Why not do it while things seem to clicking for me. Henri will be suited up and on the bench if I screw it up," Fox said with a forced shrug.

Fox could see Tremblay's lips pressed together, and he knew Coach wasn't buying his bravado bullshit, but at least the man wasn't calling him out on it.

"Then I'll let Henri and the others know, and you'll be on the roster for tomorrow afternoon," Coach Tremblay told him. "You don't have to go announcing it to the world, but if there are people you'd like to have there, I'd give them a call and then talk to the folks in the front office. They should be able to get you tickets for one of the boxes."

"Okay," Fox said, letting a grin sneak through. "Thanks, Coach." He turned to head to the locker room. A few guys in the room remarked on his accomplishment during practice, which was a nice change from the sympathetic looks and murmurs of condolence following the announcement of his father's illness. Even Martin, Gerry, and Dougie had made attempts at apologies following that revelation.

Martin cleared his throat. "I was going to head to the restaurant to apologize to your friend. I was an asshole."

"She actually quit," Fox said.

Martin frowned. "Shit, I hope it wasn't over what I said to her that night." He groaned. "I swear, I don't remember. But I know I was mouthing off."

"You weren't the reason, Martin, but she told me what you said. And yes, it was that bad," Fox assured him. "She's working with Echo on her new line so she could stop waitressing. Dealing with guys like you is only one of the reasons she left."

"Well, next time you see her, let her know I take back whatever horrible thing I said," Martin said. "Unless she's willing."

Fox glared at his teammate. "Excuse me?"

"Sorry. Bad joke."

"Why don't you tell her yourself next time *you* see her," Fox suggested. "I'll see if I can get her to come one of the nights during the homestead."

Ideally it would be perfect if Fox could get her to agree to come the following day for his start in net. Nervous as he already was, knowing she'd be there was far more comforting than the thought of his parents being in the crowd. Of course if they were in the seats so soon after his father's medical announcement, Fox knew the pressure he would wind up putting on himself would be difficult to manage.

Most of the other guys had already finished showering, so by the time Fox was finished, he had the locker room almost entirely to himself. He was pretty sure Sasha would either be between classes or at Echo's design studio for a fitting or something, so he figured he should go ahead and take the risk of asking her if she'd be interested in coming to see him play.

He could invite her to dinner afterwards. His parents would probably want to do something like that, but they'd be okay with him bringing Sasha along. It could be a way of showing her that he was interested in making things between them more official. That he was comfortable with her in a situation where his parents would undoubtedly ask questions.

Fox switched on his phone and started looking through his messages and emails. Would it be better to call his parents or Sasha first? He knew he'd rather talk to Sasha, but talking with her could be like a reward for dealing with his parents.

He smiled at the thought of Sasha as a treat for his own good behavior, and absentmindedly flicked through his email messages, looking for the pictures he'd sent himself from her phone at the party the night before.

His heart beat faster with panic when he couldn't find them. *He couldn't find them.* They weren't in his inbox. He tried a few searches but nothing came back.

Setting the phone on the bench beside him, he leaned his elbows on his thighs and rested his head in his hands, gripping his hair tightly in an effort to remember *exactly* what he'd done to her phone the night before. His memory of *taking* the pictures was crystal clear, as was every detail of what happened immediately after.

Instead of the familiar arousal usually inspired by the memory of Sasha lying naked with her legs splayed, ready and eager for him, Fox broke out into a cold sweat. His stomach felt like it couldn't decide whether to drop like a stone or climb its way out through his esophagus.

There were two possibilities he could think of for what had happened. He prayed that what he'd done was delete the email with the photos when he'd intended to send it. He'd prefer to have accidentally deleted the photos altogether than the second and more likely mistake. But the sinking feeling in his gut told him that on some level he *knew* that he'd accidentally committed an error that was far worse. It was something he'd done before, though never with something so sensitive.

He'd sent the photos to the wrong person.

His big fingers and the small touchscreens of smartphones didn't mix, and he was constantly hitting the wrong letters. He usually made a point of double-checking things before hitting the send button or confirming anything, but he still tended to receive emails in response from unintended recipients, alerting him to his error.

What made it all worse was that he'd sent the photos from Sasha's phone. On his own phone, he had the addresses and phone numbers programmed in so the chances of him hitting the wrong thing were significantly smaller. But sending them from her phone... He couldn't even go into the history to see who he'd accidentally sent them to.

The urge to vomit was strong. He dropped his head between his knees. What if she received one of those emails from some stranger wondering who she was, and why she'd sent them a bunch of nude pictures? Fuck. One of those pictures was…

He made a mad dash to the bathroom stall and got there just in time.

He'd fucking lost the intimate photos he'd taken of her — of *them*. While his face wasn't in any of them, there was one part of himself that most certainly was…and *her* face was certainly visible in several of them.

Fuck. So much for his relationship with Sasha being uncomplicated. Now it was like everything else in his life that he'd managed to sabotage. Even if she could forgive him for this level of stupidity, he knew he'd never be able to live it down. Forget having any kind of romantic relationship with her. She'd never trust him again. He was suddenly making that prick Ryan look like a damn genius. Fox couldn't even think of the guy as a prick anymore in good conscience, not when what *he'd* done was so dumb.

He picked himself off the floor and flushed the toilet, then moved to the sink to clean himself up. He couldn't call her from the locker room. And calling her from Mars was out. He could wait at home for her to return and break the news to her in person. But still that felt like the coward's way out, putting it off. Not to mention, the longer he waited to warn her and start looking into where the pictures might be, the greater the chances of the images being posted to some shady website.

He would head home and call her from the apartment. He just prayed there was some way he could undo the mistake.

Chapter Fourteen

"You're not in the middle of something involving needles and pinning fabric, are you?" Fox asked cautiously.

"No," Sasha told him. "We just got here and haven't started yet. What's up?" She glanced over her shoulder to where Echo and Jen had retreated to the other side of the room to give her privacy. She was relieved, because whatever Fox had called to say about the story, she knew there was a decent chance she was going to be upset in a way she wouldn't want them to see.

"So, I discovered something today..." he began. Sasha moved to sit down, waiting for him to start accusing her of things and calling her names she probably deserved.

"Okay..."

"When...when I went to look for those pictures of you that I sent to my phone..."

Sasha blinked, confused, before a ripple of terror skittered over her skin. The hairs on her arms stood on end, ready for the coming fight-or-flight impulse. This wasn't what she'd expected. What was going on?

"What about those pictures?" she asked

slowly.

"I don't have them."

Sasha forced herself to take a deep breath. "What do you mean, you don't have them? *Who* has them?"

He exhaled loudly on the other end. "I don't know, exactly," Fox admitted. "They're on your phone," he said, speaking quickly. "Unless you deleted them, which you probably should. And after I emailed them to myself last night, I should have checked right then and there to see if they came through. And if I'd thought to check then and there, maybe we could have stopped the message from going through or something—"

The bottom fell out of her world.

"You lost the pictures? What—? How could you do something like that to me?" Sasha exploded as the impact of what he was telling her sunk in.

"It was an accident and, to be fair, you were kind of distracting me at the time. And it was your phone instead of mine, you still don't have my email address programmed in your phone," he rambled on the other end of the line. "I'm so, so, so sorry and I'm going to do everything I can to get them back for you—"

"You can't just *get them back*," she shouted, no longer caring that Echo and Jen could hear her.

"This is the digital age—once those things are out there, they're out there forever."

"It depends on who I accidentally sent them to," he insisted. "If I can find out and get in touch with them, I might be able to convince them to just delete the photos, and it never goes beyond a few of us."

"Did you do this on purpose?" A horrible thought shook her to her core.

"What? Of course not. Why would I do it on purpose? Those pictures were supposed to be for *me* to enjoy, and I promise I won't ever try to do anything like—"

"To get back at me," Sasha interrupted. "For the story today. Did you do this to get back at me for not telling you sooner?"

"Story? What story? Sasha, this was an accident, I swear," he insisted.

"You saw that the station aired my story, and you realized it was about you and you got pissed, so you 'accidentally' lost the naked pictures of me," she said. "You're pissed at me and I get that, but... Seriously, Fox—those pictures could ruin my career. They'll undermine everything I try to do as a journalist. It'll make everything about my sex life for the rest of my life."

"You did a story about me? And you think

I'm mad at you for it?" Fox's voice sounded hollow. "What exactly did you say about me?" It seemed like he tried to laugh, but it came out as more of a choking sound.

"For the record, it's not really about you. I told them no, but they went ahead with the angle anyway," she muttered, still focused on the tarnished image of the career she'd hoped to have. "What was I supposed to do? I was working on it for my final project for my internship, and the station decided to run it today because they had a scheduling problem for a different story. It aired at noon, and it's up on the website. It's just about the pressure put on young athletes."

His voice went icy. "You did a story all about how I choke under pressure?"

Then she heard it. The hurt she'd been expecting from the beginning finally came through and dampened some of Sasha's fury over the pictures.

"It's…it's not *about* you, Fox. I swear." Sasha explained. "I just… Seeing you go through so much every time you had one of those tryouts was maybe the inspiration. But you're doing it," she emphasized. "You're doing great now with the team so…even if I got the idea because of –"

"Just stop, Sasha," he interrupted. "I'm going

to find out where those pictures ended up. If you... If you check your phone...you should be able to see in the sent mail or sent messages thing what I typed instead of my address. That...that will give me a place to start." His voice was hollow, chilled.

"Fox... I'm... I meant to tell you about the story. I never thought the station would actually *air* it, and they didn't give me much warning. I only found out this morning and when I went to your room, you'd already left for the day and—"

"You know what? Just forward it to me, okay? Forward me the typo email address, and I'll take care of it. I've gotta go." He hung up.

"Fox..." she said to the nothingness on the other end, then sighed and ended the call.

"When I told you that you should talk to him," Echo said with gentle sarcasm, "that wasn't exactly what I had in mind."

"I just...he lost some..."

"Pictures," Jen finished for her. "We heard."

"If they get out...and my boss sees them...or anyone at the station...or my *professors*..." Sasha agonized, each possibility striking her like a punch in the gut. "I'll *never* have a career. Not the one I want. And I'll never live down the...humiliation. The stigma will follow me forever."

"Well, now, let's not overreact," Echo said,

trying to calm her down. "How bad are these pictures?"

"Bad. You can't see them." Sasha said firmly.

"I can look at them for you and give you an objective opinion," Jen volunteered, taking the phone from her to flip through the pictures.

She wasn't particularly skilled at keeping a straight face while she did so, which made Sasha's face burn. When she got to the end, Jen's eyes went wide, and she pressed her lips together before turning the phone over and handing the phone back to Sasha.

"Okay, yeah," Jen said with a nod. "If those get out, it would be bad. I mean, they're tastefully shot, never would have guessed Fox had such command of lighting and an eye for composition—"

"I got it," Echo interrupted. "It's bad for Sasha if these get out."

"They could be worse. In a lot of them you can't see your face, so that's something. But that last one—the little video thing..." Jen flushed.

"Oh, God!" Sasha moaned, as the clip in question began playing. She had visions of that clip splashed across the internet with gossip articles about how she was spreading her legs for the Coulter connections Fox had to offer. Something that her work with Echo would only appear to confirm. Headlines about how many different ways she could bend her body to the Coulters' advantage. She'd be reviled. Called a gold-digger, a sell-out. The thought of Ryan's reaction. The vindication he would feel, and the superiority he would project when he found out that she was fucking Fox.

Thinking about how her family would react was actually worse, because she knew her father would see it as her big opportunity. He'd probably make some comment about how getting Fox to knock her up and marry her would set her up for life. Her stomach rolled.

"So let's see who he sent them to instead of himself," Jen said, pushing the hand Sasha held the phone in up toward her face. "Forward him the address and he can contact them, or you can reach out to them directly and explain what happened and appeal to their sense of decency."

"This is *not* how I wanted to make my name in the industry," Sasha whispered, feeling too defeated to say much more.

"When did Fox try sending the photos to himself?" Echo asked, her brow furrowed.

"Well," Sasha cleared her throat. "He took them while we were at a party last night. As soon as…as soon as we were *done* and were getting dressed again," she had to look away as she continued, "he realized that the phone he'd grabbed was mine and not his. So he took my phone and sent them to…whomever."

"It looks like he might've sent them to another Coulter," Jen remarked as she peered at the phone.

"Oh, God," Sasha groaned. "Who? Please God, not your grandfather."

"It doesn't matter," Echo insisted. Sasha was inclined to agree with the statement until she realized Echo meant something else by it.

"What are you talking about? Of course it matters. It's humiliating."

"Well, yeah, it is all that," Echo agreed. "But if Fox sent the photos last night, and it's the middle of the day today… Okay, *maybe* it would take longer than that for the photos to become a big thing, but the longer you *don't* hear about it from anyone except Fox, the better the chances are that whoever he sent them to is going to sit on them and make sure they don't get out. If he accidentally sent them to someone in the family, they'll almost certainly keep it to themselves," Echo insisted.

"It's Dax's address, by the looks of things." Jen jumped in, pointing at the screen. "Fox probably just hit the 'D' instead of the 'F' when he was typing it in."

"You guys all have email addresses through the company?" Sasha asked Echo. "Are they routed through the same server? Do you know if anyone else in the company has the ability to access things like that if they're shared?" She was beginning to panic again at the sight of the Legacy Sports domain name on the end of the email address.

"One step at a time," Echo said in as calming a tone as she could manage. "We'll take care of this and make sure they don't go any further. Send that message to Fox, and I'll give him a call and make sure he knows what he's doing in terms of handling this. We'll help you."

Chapter Fifteen

Fox wasn't sure Sasha would send him the email address at all — she didn't sound like she trusted him to do much of anything anymore, and given the stupidity of the mistake he'd made, he wasn't sure he blamed her.

What killed him was that she thought he had purposely sent the photos as some sort of revenge against her. If she'd just told him the direction of the story, he wouldn't have been too worried about it. Curious and a little self-conscious, sure, but not worried. He trusted her and her judgment. She'd always looked out for him.

But the way she reacted and got defensive about her story...*that* had him worried. He sat on his bed and reached for his computer, opening up a browser and searching for Sasha's name, silently praying that the photos wouldn't appear in the results. There were quite a few hits, most of them linking back to the station's homepage, and the video with Sasha's story.

After taking a deep breath, he clicked play and watched the video. It was longer than he'd thought it would be, and he listened to the way she spoke about the struggles of washed-up athletes who had seemingly wasted their lives, only to choke and fail at the moment of truth and fade into obscurity. When the story ended, he clicked to watch it again.

His phone vibrated, indicating a message had come through, but he ignored it.

This was what Sasha had been working on for the last several weeks. All the times he'd confided in her. When he thought there was something wrong with him. The fact that he had considered going to a special therapist because he was worried at some level he was doing it on purpose, the thoughts he'd confessed to having that made him feel like a horrible person. And she'd listened quietly, reassuring him.

But really, *this* was what had been going through her mind. She didn't believe in him, she *pitied* him. When she was encouraging him to keep going, had it just been some kind of experiment to see how far he would go? What it would take to break him? Was she just looking for more material?

She must have been. That was the only reason he could think of for why she hadn't just told him about it sooner. If she'd said it when the idea first occurred to her, he probably would have laughed about it with her and told her to go for it. But she'd hidden it from him. Lied to him about it. She thought he would be mad enough to leak naked pictures of her for revenge, which meant she thought he *should* be that mad. The more he thought about it, the more hurt he was, and more convinced she had been using him.

When the phone rang and he saw it was Echo calling, he ignored that call as well. She was with Sasha and was probably checking up on him to scold him about the pictures. She'd probably seen Sasha's news piece by now and knew the truth. Each time he watched it, it was increasingly obvious.

The next time the phone rang, it was Dax calling. There was a chance Echo had put him up to it, but he might also have just seen Sasha's story and want to check in on how his infamous loser of a younger brother was handling the taste of fame he'd been given.

"What, Dax?" Fox answered, his voice devoid of emotion.

"If you wanted to let the family know you and Sasha Tenison were a thing now, you could have just said it," his older brother teased. "We would have believed you. You didn't have to send us photographic proof."

Fox froze. "I sent the pictures to you?" His desperation to rectify his earlier mistake temporarily overpowered the disgust he'd been feeling for Sasha and the tactical move that suggested she was willing to sacrifice their friendship for the sake of her career.

"Hadn't checked my email until I got a call from Echo a few minutes ago. She said *someone* hit the 'D' instead of the 'F' when they were trying to email the pictures to you."

Fuck, had Dax looked at them?

"Delete them. Please," Fox begged. "Just…get rid of them, whatever you do."

"Already done. I can get you in touch with the IT guy who handles the company server the emails get routed through. He's had to help me out with something like this before. Don't…ask," Dax added. "Just…he's a good guy. He'll walk you through the steps so you can take care of it yourself, and he never has to see or be tempted or anything like that."

"Thanks. I'll give him a call," Fox said. Some of the tension melted away, but he knew it wouldn't fade completely until the photo situation was entirely in hand.

"No problem. And, uh…if you're going to go digital, don't do it on your cell phone. Use a camera where you can print off a few copies to stick in an old photo album or something and then delete them off the memory card. Nothing with the internet,"

Dax advised. "Just, you know…I heard it from a friend."

"Oh, there will be no next time on this one," said Fox.

"She'll get over it, Fox," Dax assured him. "Just give it some time and she'll—"

"That's *not* why there won't be a next time. Have you seen the story she did that aired today?"

"I thought Sasha was still in school?"

"She's doing an internship at TVN and had to put a piece together for a project. They liked hers enough to air it. You should check it out before telling me about the mistake *I* made." With the photo situation almost resolved, anger returned as his primary emotion, making him fume over Sasha's betrayal. "Oh, and Coach wants me to start tomorrow's home game," he added. "Let me know if you'll be around and want tickets." He hung up on Dax before his brother could reply.

A few minutes later, Dax sent the phone number for the company IT guy, along with a confirmation that he would like to see his little brother in net the next day.

***

Sasha was much calmer after Echo talked to Dax. He promised to delete it immediately, and he assured Echo that the company's IT guy would be able to clear it off the server.

"Now that that's settled, do we think we can focus on this fitting?" Echo asked after hanging up the phone.

They were quieter than usual as they bustled about to get Sasha into the newly redesigned runner's outfit in the new fabric. Jen made notations according to Echo's dictation and grabbed the things Echo needed that weren't close at hand.

"I want you to raise your arms like this," Echo instructed and demonstrated, running through a number of movements for Sasha to attempt and report on how it felt to perform them in the new clothes.

Once the preliminaries were taken care of, Jen brought out a camera so they could get a few shots of the completed outfit to go over with the photographer and makeup crew so they could prep for the photo shoot the following week. Sasha's eyes fell on the camera, and she felt herself flush.

"Just...keep the clothes on, okay?" Jen teased, lightening the mood a bit.

Sasha rolled her eyes.

Echo directed Sasha's movements and body position once more, while Jen was in charge of taking the pictures.

Each time the camera flashed, Sasha's breath

hitched a little. Shame washed over her. She'd hurt him. The one person she'd loved since she was a kid. She'd hurt him. The things she'd said on the phone...the story. It was a mistake that could have happened to anyone, and he had immediately called to tell her everything and apologize. And what had she done? She'd chewed him out over it. Worse, she'd accused him of doing it *on purpose*. The guilt she felt about the story she'd done...she'd taken the anger she had toward herself and redirected it at Fox.

"Could you try to look a little less...distraught?" Jen called.

Echo elbowed her friend. "It doesn't matter for these," she said to Sasha, rolling her eyes. "Give her a break."

"Sorry," Sasha said, trying to get her head back to the present. "She's right. Even if the proper shoot isn't until next week, it's not like I can't practice." She blinked and shook herself out before turning to face Jen and the camera, striking a pose.

But her thoughts wouldn't be controlled so easily. They drifted back to the night before and posing for Fox. The way his face lit up as she shifted on the bed, teasing him as she draped the fabric of her skirt across her body to conceal and reveal the intimate spaces she shared with him. The way he'd made a show of each piece of clothing as he removed it in payment for the next picture. The warmth that had flooded through her, even as her skin broke out in goose bumps.

No, she didn't regret those photographs. She hadn't even deleted them from her phone yet. Not even their short sex tape. A whole new wave of guilt crashed over her at the thought of how she'd blown her opportunity to come clean with him. She'd definitely blown her chance at having more with him. She'd been so scared to admit she wanted it, so scared of losing the friendship they already had, that she might well have lost it all.

Her phone rang, and Echo grabbed it for her.

"Fox," she mouthed, handing it over and then grabbing Jen to pull her away and give Sasha some privacy.

"Look, the photo thing is all taken care of," he said curtly when she answered. "No traces of them left anywhere along the chain, including the email server, and Dax swore to me that he deleted his. The only ones left, if you haven't deleted them already, are the ones on your phone."

"I'm sorry," Sasha said quickly. "About how I reacted before, and about the story." He didn't hang up, but he didn't say anything either, so she continued. "I meant to tell you sooner. I *should* have told you sooner. And it doesn't matter that I didn't think they'd ever air it or whatever…I still should have talked to you about it."

"I think you were pretty thorough," he responded with no trace of sympathy or forgiveness in his voice. "I don't think I could have added anything more to it, if you had been looking for more input."

"Input? Fox…you know that's not what I meant. That's not why I wanted to do the story at all." Sasha tried to defend herself, but couldn't get mad about what he said. His disgust was justified, and she should just take it. "I wasn't trying to use you. You know I would never do that." Her voice was low because she couldn't suppress the wavering in it if she spoke any louder, and the last thing she wanted was to cry. Things would be even worseif he thought she was manipulating him.

"I used to think that, but now… You *know* how much I hate being pitied, and yet… Being pitied by people you thought were your friends is so much worse than being pitied by strangers. At least if Coach Tremblay gave me this chance on the team because he pitied me, I can tell myself that he doesn't really know me. But you… You know me better than anyone."

Tears streamed down her cheeks.

"Coach Tremblay doesn't pity you, and *I* certainly don't. I *know* how great you are in goal, and I know how hard you try—"

"But you know it's not enough—and you're right. Maybe it's my own fault for complaining about it all the time. You did say you were tired of stroking egos, and what was I doing with all that complaining about myself-doubt if it wasn't looking for you to give me a solid boost, huh?"

"Stop it, Fox," she said firmly. "I said I was sorry for not coming to you about the story sooner. I was afraid you'd do something like this—let it bother you and make you doubt yourself."

"Give me an excuse for when I inevitably fail?"

"You're not going to fail."

"I don't believe you. After all, I can't even send myself an email without screwing it up."

"It was a mistake, and I'm sorry for how I reacted," she repeated. "I was surprised and scared and took my fear out on you. You did the right thing by telling me what happened and you've handled it, and now I'm sorry I made such a big deal out of the whole thing."

"It *is* a big deal. You can't trust me to do anything," he said with such conviction Sasha felt his self-loathing like a punch to the chest.

"Stop saying things like that," she requested again. "I wish we could go back a day. Go back to the way things were at the party. I...I liked the way things were between us then."

"Before I screwed things up with the pictures?"

"Forget about the pictures," she snapped. "I'm sorry, okay? I'm...I'm screwing this up, I know, but I'm trying...trying to say that...I liked being with you, and..." She took a deep breath and forced the words out. "I want...to be with you—not just *be* with you like...sex." She began to ramble as she struggled to put what she wanted into words. "Not that I'm complaining about the sex. What I'm trying to say is...I love you, Fox. I'm *so* sorry for how I handled that story, but...I don't want to lose you over it. Please...*please*...forgive me..."

There was a pause from his end of the line that was eventually replaced with complete silence.

Sasha looked at the phone in disbelief, unsure what to make of his lack of reply. Then she gave in to her sobs.

Chapter Sixteen

Echo and Jen had insisted Sasha crash on their couch. They'd overheard enough of her conversation with Fox to know it would be uncomfortable for Sasha to go home to the apartment she shared with him. Her classes had been cancelled for the next day, and the last thing she needed was to be in Fox's face. She didn't have to be at the station until later in the afternoon, and she was dreading that as much as facing Fox. There were a number of congratulatory emails from the staff for how well her story was being received by both the audience and the network's higher ups. There were even plans to release segment two. But it was too late for that now.

She'd even received a civil message of congratulations from Ryan. Which was surprising. She hadn't heard from him, except through the wary stares of his immediate colleagues in the film editing departments. Sasha had managed to avoid running into him at the station...though he might have been making just as much of an effort to avoid an encounter with *her*. His email made her want to gag with his forced words of encouragement. *You'll be sure to get an offer before your internship is up... They'd have to be crazy to let you slip through their fingers.*

It was something Fox would have said once, but with sincerity.

A bunch of us want to treat you to a dinner somewhere nice to celebrate – don't worry, I already made sure we ruled out that place you used to work. She wondered if Ryan even remembered the name of the restaurant she'd worked at for four years. *Looking forward to seeing you, and congratulating you in person. I've missed you, and maybe we can find some time tomorrow to talk, just the two of us.*

The last thing she wanted was to talk alone with Ryan…or maybe it was the second-to-last thing she wanted. No, it was definitely last, because as much as she dreaded facing Fox and figuring out if they could even be friends moving forward, she longed to talk to him about Ryan's message and hear him call Ryan a prick and hypocrite.

She still felt like a horrible person when she roused herself to join Echo and Jen in the kitchen for coffee, but the promise of caffeine assured her she would be able to survive the day — even if it involved Ryan.

As it turned out, it wasn't Echo and *Jen* she'd heard stirring in the kitchen, but rather Echo and her boyfriend, Cole. She was busy measuring out scoops of ground coffee into the filter while he stood behind her, shirtless with his hands on her hips, kissing her neck. From his profile alone, Sasha couldn't help but stare for a moment. He was awfully pretty.

"Oh," Sasha blurted, startling them all the same. "Sorry. I, uh…I'll just…go take a shower…" she muttered.

"It's all right, Sash," Echo assured her, amusement in her voice. "We're behaving, I promise."

There was a low murmur from Cole that earned him a playful slap from Echo. He took over prepping the coffee machine, glancing over his shoulder to greet Sasha with a brief smile but keeping his body turned away from her. She'd seen Fox do the same thing enough times to recognize and appreciate his attempts to conceal his morning wood. Echo flew into distraction mode, ushering Sasha over to a cabinet where she could pick from several breakfast cereals.

"Have you heard anything from Fox?" Sasha made herself ask.

"No," Echo admitted. "But Dax said he and Asha are going to Fox's game today. He's going to try to talk to him. I mean…from an objective perspective, the story you did is great. And I'm sure Fox wouldn't want you to compromise your skill or the possibilities for your future by *not* doing a story just because it was uncomfortable for him. It's your job."

"I know, and that's exactly why I should have just told him about it before," Sasha reiterated as she poured Corn Flakes into the bowl Echo had retrieved for her. "But I blew it. Both with my timing and with *how* I told him."

"Now that he's had some time to let it all sink in, I think he'll be over being angry and hurt," Echo said with forced optimism, pulling open a drawer and grabbing Sasha a spoon. "Dax'll help talk him around. If you don't *know* that Fox was what inspired that story, you wouldn't be able to tell just by watching it. Sure there's some footage of him, but he's not the main focus. The story shows some tryouts, a win, and a defeat, but your footage focuses mainly on the teenaged athletes."

"I know, I know," Sasha spoke around the food in her mouth. "I felt so guilty the whole time I was working on it. I made sure to keep the content as far away from Fox as possible while constructing it."

"My guess is, he'll be over it once the game today is done," Echo shrugged. "Fox is sensitive about his playing, so you struck a nerve, but he's never been one to hold a grudge like that. And he's never been able to stay mad at you. Not even that time you broke his favorite stick."

Sasha smiled reflexively at the memory. Fox had been teaching her to play hockey, so he'd have someone who could take shots on him and help him practice. She'd requested a rest from the endless skating that came with having to shoot the puck at him repeatedly and asked that they swap positions. Relenting, he'd handed over his custom goalie stick for her to use before taking her stick and skating off to retrieve the puck. About fifteen minutes later, he'd tried a fancy spinning move to get the puck in, but their skates had gotten tangled and he'd fallen on top of her with his stick breaking her fall.

"I hope we can get back to where we were in our friendship," Sasha agreed. "But I don't know that I can handle trying to be...*more* than that. I mean, I told him I loved him. And he hung up on me. Now it'll be this *thing* between us. I'm that girl."

Echo refrained from commenting, filling her mouth with a piece of toast. Sasha finished her Corn Flakes in silence before glancing at the clock.

"I should head home and change," she said. "Fox should've headed out for his pregame practice by now."

"Are you interested in going to the game?" Echo asked. "My parents are going with Dax and

Asha, and us. They got some private box through the team. I'm sure they could get you in, too."

"I don't think he'd want me there. I'll watch at the station. The sports guys will have it on so they can write something up for tonight and note the video clips they have to request from the league."

"Going to the game in person could get you out of that work thing," Echo pointed out.

"No, they'd just postpone it. I think I've done enough postponing things because they'd be uncomfortable," Sasha muttered.

"Well, if you want to crash here again tonight, just shoot me a text or give me a call. And I'll leave a ticket, just in case you change your mind."

"Thanks, Echo." Sasha nodded appreciatively before turning her attention to Cole. "It was nice to meet you." She headed for the living room and gathered her things before trudging to her car and driving over to her empty apartment. She had to get ready for work at the station and prepare herself to watch and pray that her conversation with Fox didn't send him into a tailspin on the ice.

Chapter Seventeen

Sasha's words kept playing over and over in Fox's mind. She loved him. What was he supposed to do with that? He kept himself locked in his room, considering heading out for the night and maybe avoiding coming home again. He didn't want to have to worry about seeing her in the apartment and confronting her the minute she walked through the door. Confronting her with what, he wasn't sure. He couldn't think of anything to say that he hadn't already said — except that he forgave her, but he wasn't ready for that yet. If she'd told him she loved him *before*…

He flopped back on his bed to stare at the ceiling. He couldn't deal with it right now. With what might have been between him and Sasha. That was the whole reason *he* hadn't brought up a hypothetical relationship to see if she'd be receptive. He had wanted it, but knew she *didn't*. It was what she'd said when she broke up with Ryan.

And now there was just too much that he needed to focus on for himself. He was starting in net for his first home game in a little less than fifteen hours. He should be preparing for that.

He pulled over his laptop and started going through video of the players from Philadelphia, the ones who would be taking their shots on him during the upcoming game. Sitting on his bed, he mimed the moves he would make to block various shots. He analyzed the players for tics that would show which direction they might come at him and where they'd try to sneak the puck through. He looked for passing patterns among the players on various lines. And in the back of his mind, he kept one ear trained on the apartment door and the first hint of it opening.

When he finally couldn't focus on the screen anymore and shut the laptop down, he ventured from his room to see if he'd missed her, but she was nowhere in the apartment. She had to be avoiding him, and he was too tired to think about whether that supported or undermined her declaration of her feelings for him. He locked everything up, turned the lights out, and went to bed.

She might have been avoiding him in the waking world, but he found her in his dreams. He was back on the floor of the shower with her sitting there beside him. Only this time, they were both naked. The failure weighed heavy on him as she brought his head down to rest against her shoulder, stroking his wet hair back as the water sluiced over them both.

He couldn't understand exactly what she was saying, but it was gentle and soothing. She dipped her head to press a kiss to his brow, then his closed eyes, and finally his mouth.

The spike of heat was instant, and he reached up to cup the back of her head, holding her lips and her tongue hostage to his own. Her hand dropped to his dick and stroked him gently before she broke away from him and straddled him. His cock slid easily inside her, and she rode him hard, her hands pressing down on his chest, and the water spraying him in the face.

He couldn't get the water out of his face. Couldn't see her as she rose and fell above him. He sought the eye contact they usually had when they made love, but the water prevented that. He tried wiping his face to clear his mouth and nose as he started to choke on the water. But he could only manage long enough to cough and have it all fill again. He grabbed a tighter hold of her waist and pulled himself upright, sputtering as he rolled her onto her back so the water would strike his shoulderblades and he could leverage himself to thrust inside her and push them both to the brink of release. As he rose above her, however, she cried out with pleasure and dissolved beneath him.

He woke with a start and groaned at the fleeting sensations that had been so vivid in his dream. But he felt drained and used. He was too tired and not in the mood to analyze his dreams that deeply. He settled for being relieved that she hadn't come home, that he didn't have to face her yet, and he dreaded when both would be necessary.

After the disturbing dream he'd had, Fox opted out of showering at the apartment and headed to the rink early to get in a bit of extra practice before the game. His brain wouldn't let it go, though. He found himself checking his phone to see if he had any messages or missed calls from her, even as he told himself he wasn't ready and didn't want to hear from her. *Stop being a pussy and focus.*

Coming off the ice to head down to the locker room for the pregame coaching session and associated rituals, his teammates and coaches were enthusiastic about his fast-approaching start.

"Your family here for the game?" Henri asked in a hoarse voice as he popped a cough drop into his mouth and noisily cleared his throat and nose.

"Uh…yeah, I think so," Fox said with a shrug. He turned to his phone and realized that he had received several texts from Dax stating that he and their parents had been able to pick up the tickets that had been left for them with the front office without incident. Asha, Dax's girlfriend, had apparently come as well, and was busy chatting with some old college friends of hers in the media booth. All the messages showed as having been read by Fox, but he honestly couldn't remember reading a single one of them. "Yup, sounds like they're settled in their box. What about you? Did you get any of your family over for your first home game?"

Henri nodded but it dislodged something in his sinuses, and he turned to sneeze into a towel hanging in his locker. Fox took three steps away while Henri's back was turned. If he got sick, too, the team would be completely screwed in goal.

"Well, uh, any advice?" Fox asked as they got the call to line up for their introduction and official warmup skate in front of the fans before puck drop.

Henri scrunched his face in thought before shrugging and responding, "Stop the puck."

"Thanks," Fox gave a nervous laugh as he made his way to the end of the line. "That's, uh, helpful."

That was the last clear thing Fox could make out as the noise of the crowd overwhelmed him, and he moved to the bench for the game's opening ceremonies. Even the singing of the national anthem was fuzzy in his ears. He headed for the crease when the rest of his starting teammates climbed over the boards. After a few moments of roughing up the ice in the crease, he had it just the way he liked it and settled in, determined to focus on the game.

And he did. Fox saw every move that happened in front of him and felt his body reacting. He was completely aware of where the puck was at every moment, ignoring the calls between the players on the ice and the pounding noise of the fans against the Plexiglas barrier behind him.

But at the same time, he wasn't actively thinking about the game, only reacting to it. Consciously, he was struggling to keep thoughts of Sasha and the story she'd done at bay. Snippets of her voiceover came back to him when the puck was down at the other end of the rink. *We see and hear so much in the media about those who have defied the odds and made it to the big leagues… But what about those who have the odds deliberately stacked in their favor? There are plenty of them, as well. All of those players working undeniably hard to earn and keep their prominent positions. And then there are those whose names we never learn. Those whose talents and efforts come to naught.*

He was never mentioned by name in her piece, undeniably by Sasha's design. But what her motivations were for keeping him out of it…

"Great period, man." One of the defensemen slapped Fox's padded shoulder. Fox realized he hadn't even heard the buzzer. He followed Jones off the ice. Had it really been a full twenty minutes of play? He hadn't let a single shot in. He knew that much, but he wasn't sure how many shots had come at him to begin with. The puck had spent a while down the other end of the ice, of that, he was certain. There were two or three specific saves he remembered, and one sore spot on his thigh where a puck had hit him a bit higher than his goalie pads extended. Not so hard a hit as to cause serious damage, just an annoying twinge that would bruise later.

Coach Tremblay was pleased, but didn't make a big deal of how he'd done in the first period. They were up one to nothing, and he wanted to widen that gap in the next twenty minutes so he focused most of his attention on the forwards, drawing a few approaching formations for them on his dry-erase clipboard. The intermission was over all too quickly, and they were headed back out to the ice. Coach Tremblay gave him a knock on his helmet and a low, "Keep it up, Coulter."

The second period passed in much the same manner as the first. Fox's thoughts continued to slip toward Sasha. Was she watching the game? She'd been so excited over the way he'd played in his first game with the team, but would she even talk to him after this one? Would she kick him out of the apartment?

If her story got picked up when she didn't even consider it finished, that had to mean the station would offer her a job when her internship was up and she had graduated. She wouldn't need his help to pay the rent after that. Not to mention her modeling job for Echo — the campaign, or whatever it was called — hadn't officially launched, but Echo was excited about it. Sasha would be too important for him, even if he was a Coulter.

The other team's offense was definitely down his end of the ice more during the second period. They weren't spending as much time passing between themselves to set up the perfect shot. No, they were just trying to pummel him, hoping he'd let something slip through. There was a looseness, strength, and speed Fox was able to channel in a way he hadn't managed to coordinate effectively in the past. It was as though he almost wasn't there; as though he were watching idly from the sidelines as someone else played goalie. He knew what he had to do for his team, but it didn't intimidate him the way he so often let it in the past. Besides, nothing would be as humiliating as what he'd felt watching Sasha's story about 'those who have every advantage, including talent, but who cannot overcome themselves' as she'd put it, and *knowing* that she'd been thinking specifically of him when she wrote those words.

He wished he didn't care what she thought of him, but the memory of the raw desire in her eyes told him otherwise. Those green orbs mesmerized him as they changed from hazel to something almost emerald, depending on the light. He wanted her to look at him like that again. But he didn't know if maybe he'd imagined all of that. Maybe he'd only ever seen what he wanted to see as far as Sasha was concerned.

Fox threw himself to the ice in an uncomfortable split, his glove hand reaching desperately behind his leg to cover the puck just as it reached the blue line. Suddenly, he was bowled over by one of his teammates and one of the other team's forwards as they collided and landed on top of him and his stick arm.

He heard something snap and a lot of whistles blowing as the refs came over to untangle the mess of players and sort out the necessary penalties. Fox heard one of the other team's players shouting about how the puck had crossed the line and Fox had drawn it back over before it registered and the buzzer could sound the goal. But when the ref looked to Fox's gloved hand, Fox raised it and the puck was sitting on the right side of the line. No goal. When the other team's coach pushed for a review, Fox used the intervening minutes to stretch himself out and skate to the bench for a replacement stick. He was lucky it was his stick and not his arm that had snapped when the two tangled players came down on him.

The challenge went in the Brawlers' favor. No goal.

The second period came to an end a few minutes later, with the Brawlers up three to nothing.

"You sure this is your first game on home ice?" One of the guys joked with Fox as they made their way down the tunnel for the second intermission.

"Local network wants to do an interview with you during the break," Martin whispered with an elbow nudge. But before Fox could even consider panicking, Martin laughed. "Don't worry. The coaches don't want you getting distracted in the middle of the game like that. They'll save you for the post-game press conference. It'll be one the assistant coaches this time. Tremblay wants us pushing our advantage in the third. Here's hoping that lost challenge keeps them down instead of riling them up again."

Fox's instructions for the third period consisted of, "keep doing what you've been doing." And he did, closing the game with a shutout, the Brawlers winning five to nothing. At the end of the game, the arena's announcers called him out to take a special bow as they congratulated him on finishing his second NHL start, his first at-home start, and his first shutout game. The fans screamed and applauded as his stats for the game were read aloud, including thirty-six blocked shots on goal.

Holy fuck. He'd done far better than he'd ever imagined. He'd mostly hoped to keep from embarrassing himself in net. *Maybe* pull off enough blocked shots to help the team win. But a shutout... As he headed back off the ice to go down the tunnel to the locker room, he spotted his parents, grandparents, Echo, Cole, Dax, and Asha in a private box waving and cheering.

Flashes from cameras and shouts from fans followed him as he left the ice. Voices echoed through the concrete halls leading out from the locker room, and he heard his name tossing about in the mix. Coach Tremblay stopped him just inside the locker-room door to shake his hand.

"You did great out there, Coulter. Head office is already working on formalizing an offer for you for that second spot. Keep a watch out for a call from your agent. Oh, and uh, it *might* come up at the press conference. Shower quick. They're going to want to talk to you."

Standing in the stream of hot water, Fox's mind returned once more to Sasha. He felt numb. He should be excited about the contract he was going to be offered and feeling more secure. He wasn't going to be going back down to the farm system any time soon. And what's more, he hadn't just been decent in his first home game, he'd dominated the net. The only person he wanted to call was Sasha. She was the only person he could trust to be properly excited by the news. But the lingering disappointment in her left him feeling cold with a pit in his stomach. He failed at convincing himself it was just nerves for the press conference, instead, giving himself *actual* nerves. Would any of them ask questions about Sasha's piece? It had been circulating for more than a full day now, and there was certainly evidence to point to him as the source of inspiration.

He turned off the water and shook his head to clear it, then ran his hands through his hair to squeeze out the extra water. Maybe he was being too harsh on her. She hadn't mentioned him by name, and it would take some digging for someone to find their connection to one another if they didn't know to look for it.

Throwing his clothes on, he winced. He was sore from some of those saves. The bruise on his thigh was blooming nicely, too. He was also exhausted. Physically, mentally, and emotionally. He didn't want to keep forcing himself to be mad at Sasha for what she'd done. Or hadn't done. It was still a disorganized mess. And she had apologized. He'd done something incredibly stupid himself, and she appeared to have forgiven him. Fuck, if those photos had made their way out into the public, it could have been a hundred times worse for her career than anyone finding out he'd inspired her story would be for his. She had only said some of the things she said because she was terrified, and with good reason.

She would never do anything to consciously hurt him...except she *had* done that story...but she'd apologized for not telling him. Didn't that show she *was* concerned about how he felt? Or was she simply trying to make herself feel better after the fact?

The real question was, could he believe her?

"Hurry up, Coulter." Someone he didn't recognize was urging him toward the door to the pressroom. She wore a loose-fitting pantsuit and held a clipboard, so she was probably someone associated with the team's PR group. She stopped him for a minute to give him a quick inspection and tucked in the tag at the back of his shirt. Then she nodded and nudged him out into the room where the press was seated with their cameras pointed at him, waiting.

***

Fox's teammates were mostly gone by the time he finished up with the press conference, and the arena had emptied of fans. Only a few had been allowed by security to remain behind. When he emerged with his things, his parents and some of his siblings and their partners were waiting to congratulate him.

"Not bad, little bro." Dax smacked him on the shoulder with more force than was necessary. "Had me worried there during some of those penalty kills. Don't know how you stand the pressure when they come at you firing like that."

"The pads help." Fox joked as he hugged his mother and father.

"Really proud of you." Echo beamed, as she launched herself at him. He caught his sister easily and squeezed her tight. Cole's greeting was more subdued, but still happy as he clapped Fox on the back.

"Gage was impressed," their mother told him. "Your father's phone was going off every few seconds with text messages from him."

"I put my phone off during the game," Dax said. "Switched it back on and I had about twenty messages from Bryce."

"You did well, son," Brent Coulter said with a quiet steadiness and a light squeeze to Fox's shoulder. Shit, it was good to see him.

"That was good today. Imagine what you could do with another sport," said Gramps.

Fox didn't take it personally. He just rolled his eyes.

Gramps had a knack for making everyone around him feel childish, if only because of how his own adolescent, provoking nature inspired them to react.

"I wonder where Sasha went," His mother took his father's arm and started leading the group slowly out of the private box. "She sat with us."

Fox's gaze darted to Dax who shook his head to convey that he'd said nothing.

"You know Sasha, she had to be here for Fox, but then she had to run to work," Echo explained, even as she slid him some serious side-eye.

"She just had her first story air for the station she works with," Dax spoke up, his gaze fixed on his younger brother. "Here…let me pull it up on my phone. Echo sent it to me." Dax played the story for their parents while Fox fought the urge to smack his brother in the back of the head.

"It's really well done," Asha commented when the clip was over. "The narrative flows well, and she had someone who knew what they were doing helping with the camera angles and editing."

"She must be so excited, Fox." Julia said with a proud smile. "She did this for an internship? And it got picked to air? That's impressive. I wonder why she didn't say anything."

"Sasha is all about Fox when he plays. Every superstitious thing you can think of, she does. Everything she's ever done for any of his games that has worked. She wasn't going to break tradition and start bragging during his big game," Echo said. "She wouldn't want the attention on her."

Fox got the message, loud and clear. Sasha had been there for him, wearing his jersey, his hat, and no doubt eating a banana during each quarter. It was something she'd done in one high school game where he'd killed it. From that point on, she did it every game.

But outside of the mentions of how proud everyone was about Sasha's accomplishment, no one else had anything to say about the content beyond the depth of research Sasha must have put into crafting it, and how well she negotiated such tricky and sensitive interviews. Asha was particularly vocal about her admiration for Sasha's talent, and she pressed Fox with questions about her prospects after graduation. She proved enough of a distraction to their parents for Fox and Dax to have a few minutes of quiet conversation between them.

"*Why* did you bring up that video?" Fox whispered.

"Do you think they wouldn't have come across it on their own? I'm surprised Gramps hadn't sent it to Dad already. You know Sasha's grandfather must've sent it to him."

"And you're trying to make sure they know she did that story about me?"

"Quit being an asshole," Dax hissed. "I said nothing about you when I was showing it to them, and obviously *they* didn't think it was about you because it really isn't. Just look at how she did it. There's absolutely no reference to you personally. And even if you *were* her inspiration as far as subject matter, you haven't fallen into the patterns she describes. Today's game proves that."

"Today's game proves nothing," Fox said. "I've had two starts — that's hardly — "

"You've started with two wins, and one of them was a particularly impressive one," Dax interrupted. "From the look on your coach's face, he was pleased with how you did. There's no way that Henri guy can take a long string of consecutive starts. Not the way your old goalie could. So they're not going to be sending you back down any time soon." He leaned closer to Fox and whispered loudly, "And if what Asha overheard when she was chatting with her contacts in the PR group is true, you're going to be offered a decent contract pretty soon."

Fox rolled his eyes at the smirk on Dax's face. "That doesn't change — "

"Oh, get over yourself already and make up with Sasha. Or is she still pissed at you for that — " he looked around and spoke even quieter than he already was " — photo mix-up? I told Echo to tell her that I didn't even look at them, but if you want me to tell her that myself, just let me know. You two seemed to have a good thing going. Don't screw it up."

"There was nothing to screw up. And if there was, I already did it. She said when she broke up with her last boyfriend and kicked him out that she didn't want a relationship. They're distracting, and time consuming, and just... She was right. I need to focus on my playing — I've done well, and I need to keep going if — "

"If what? You're where you want to be, and a big part of that is because you've had Sasha supporting you."

"They're offering me that contract because I had some good games. What if I fuck up?"

"They've had their eyes on you for this position for a while," Dax reminded him. "You've had some good games, but you've also had good practices and good numbers for the team you were on. You're improving because you've been able to think beyond the ice for a while. Trust me, Fox—Sasha has been helping you. You're more relaxed when you get to see her and spend time with her." He held up his hands. "*Whatever* capacity that may be, I don't need the juicy details or any more photos. You're more sure of yourself. Don't blow that because you're too stupid to apologize and tell her how you feel."

"She... she said..." But Fox couldn't bring himself to voice it aloud to his brother.

"What do you say, Fox?" their father said, breaking into their conversation.

"What do I say to what?"

"We want to take you out to dinner to celebrate," their mother reiterated while Asha eyed Dax for not having paid attention.

"Actually, Mom," Dax said before Fox could open his mouth, "Fox was talking about how he's running late to meet up with Sasha. She's got some work thing she invited him to, I believe." Dax ignored Fox's glare.

"Oh, well, tell her we saw the video, and that we're thrilled for her. She's incredibly talented," his mother said. "We'll simply pick another day to treat you to dinner. Maybe some time when we can get everyone home."

"I'd like that," Fox agreed. "And thanks again for coming. It means a lot."

"Don't argue," Dax whispered in Fox's ear as they

briefly embraced before parting. "Just go and talk to her."

Maybe Dax was right. He headed toward the player's exit, when someone called out to him.

"Hey, Fox."

Fox stopped short at the sight of the bleached blonde in front of him. She had big tits and a smooth, flat belly. She wore a short skirt that barely covered her ass, if it did at all. *This* was his usual type. Not that he preferred this type, but it was what was usually available. And given he wasn't usually much into having deep conversations, it had worked. But not anymore. Someone had to work hard to impress him now. This kind of girl had zero appeal.

"Oh, hey."

She smiled up at him, putting a hand on his chest.

He sidestepped, attempting to make it down the gangway. He wanted to get to his car so he could go find Sasha. "Sorry, I have to get going."

She followed behind, her heels clicking on the cement. "You remember me, don't you?"

Damn. Had he fucked her? It was entirely possible. How many times after a game had he and the team celebrated? There were plenty of girls around all the time, just dying to latch themselves onto some future professional hockey player. "I'm sorry. I don't. What's your name again?"

She frowned and pouted those high-gloss pink lips. "I'm Jocelyn. We met about three months ago? I stayed over your place."

He vaguely remembered a blonde who'd come back to Martin's with him. Martin had gone home with the girl he'd picked up. And they'd been busy pounding the bed into the wall.

By contrast, the guest bedroom Fox had stayed in only had a mattress on the floor. Still, they had worked that mattress out. But he hadn't meant to let her stay.

"I'm sorry. I am really shitty with faces." *Oh yeah, slick.*

"It's okay. Really."

Oh, thank God. He wasn't prepared to remember her or her face, or exactly what they had been up to at Martin's place. He shot her a polite smile, scooted around her, and kept walking.

She practically had to run to keep up with him. "I just wanted to say congratulations. I remember you, and the guys were talking about when you were going to make it big. And now you have. I was thinking maybe you and I could go celebrate the game. It was really good."

He understood now. She'd watched the game, and thought, *Hey, he let me stay over. I must have been important to him, so let me attach myself and leach onto him as much as possible.*

He slowed his pace. "Look, Jocelyn. The thing is, I was a completely different guy then."

She frowned, her brows furrowing as if she was trying to comprehend his words. But still, he pressed on. "I honestly don't remember you. Which I know is terrible, and I feel bad. And, you seem like a nice girl, so I'm going to give you the truth. I'm totally into someone else." That *was* the truth. He needed to get to Sasha as soon as possible.

Jocelyn stopped walking and called after him. "So there's no chance that you'd like to have a repeat? I'm very good, and I already know what you like."

Fox had to laugh. "Thanks, but no thanks. I've got someone else in mind."

Fox

She faltered a little when they reached the opening to the parking lot, but nodded. "Okay, I get it. Is there anyone on the team that you think might be interested?"

Fox sighed. This wasn't about him, at all. She was trying to work her way up. "No, but you know what, I don't think you need any of those guys. I'm sure you can figure out life on your own."

She smiled up at him. "That might be the nicest thing anyone has ever said to me."

He certainly hoped not. But before Fox knew what was happening, she wrapped her arms around him, stood on tiptoe, and kissed him on the lips. He immediately stepped back, and she smiled at him. "Thank you. You really are very sweet." Then all he could do was turn to watch her walk away, wobbling in her heels as she did so. He used the back of his hand to wipe the sticky, gooey lip gloss off his mouth.

He hated that stuff. He preferred whatever it was that Sasha used.

When he turned back to the parking lot, his heart stopped.

Sasha was waiting for him at the end of the gangway. She had a sign that said, *Congratulations, let's go fuck. Holy shit.* He had missed her so much. But even now as she held up her sign, her face was stricken with sadness. Then she turned and walked away. Fox stood there, confused for a moment, but then realized what she'd seen.

Fuck. Jocelyn. "Sasha, wait. It's not what it looks like."

Sasha was surprisingly quick, and she wasn't encumbered by hockey gear. So she climbed into her car and was gone before Fox could catch her.

Shit. Shit. How had he gotten all of this so screwed up?

Well, are you going to feel bad for yourself, or are you going to go get your girl?

That wasn't even a question. He ran to his car and threw his stuff in the trunk. Now all he had to do was figure out where Sasha was going, because he wasn't going to let her walk away.

Fox

Chapter Eighteen

When Sasha returned to the office, Ryan was waiting at her cubicle. He was hovering near her desk when she arrived, and immediately congratulated her on the success of her story and apologized for the way he'd handled their breakup.

"We both said a lot of things we didn't mean trying to hurt each other," he said. "But now that we've had some time apart and now that you're closer to getting your degree, I think we can do better. That we can make it work and get back to the way things were between us in the beginning."

Seriously? She didn't need this shit right now. "You might have said things you didn't mean," she quipped, "but *I* meant every word. Now, unless you want me repeating a few of them for your friends to hear, leave me alone."

"Come on, Sasha," he pleaded, following her as she sat at her desk and began sorting through the leftover paperwork from her story. She decided to hold on to the sources she cited directly and have a separate file for those that had proved interesting additional reading, tossing the remaining ones in a bin to be recycled.

"Is this about the apartment? I shouldn't have bailed on it like that and left you to take care of

247

the rent on your own, okay? Your name was the only one on the lease, but you and I did have an understanding. I should've just…taken the other bedroom or something—helped you find a new roommate. If you need help with it, I'd be happy to come home again, or at least help out with the bills while we figure this out."

"There's nothing to figure out," Sasha said, continuing her attempts to ignore him. "It's taken care of."

His brows snapped down. "What the hell does that mean?"

She met his gaze directly. "It means I don't need your help financially or otherwise, and I don't want your company. I said what I needed to say when I threw you out. Now please, don't make this any more embarrassing for yourself than it needs to be," she said in a low voice. A quick glance at the clock showed the appointed hour for everyone to head out and celebrate was fast approaching. Sasha knew from previous gatherings, her colleagues would soon start congregating near her cubicle to chat and wait before heading out en masse.

"So you were fucking some other guy," Ryan muttered beneath his breath.

She knew she shouldn't have done it, but she smiled evilly and said, "Not till after I kicked you out, and that's not how I would describe it, but…yeah. There's someone I care about—more than I cared about you, if you *really* want to know the truth. I'm not sure where it's going—if anywhere—but I'm certainly not getting back together with you, so… Leave. Me. Alone." Her anger and frustration with Ryan were keeping her from crumpling at the thought of Fox and the shambles of their friendship.

Ryan clearly had more he wanted to say, and judging by the color of his face, it wasn't anything pleasant. So Sasha was thankful when Jeanine and a few others came over with their coats over their arms, ready to go.

"Everything all right?" Jeanine asked, her gaze flitting between Sasha and Ryan.

"Yeah," Sasha assured her colleague as she pushed her chair back and rose to start cleaning up her desk. "Ryan was just explaining that he had a small family emergency and can't make it tonight. His aunt's gone into the hospital and needs him to stop by her house and grab a few things for her." She stacked her piles of paperwork together to create more coherent long-term files later.

He glared at her when she looked up at him and raised her brows in a dare. If he denied her lie, she'd have an opportunity to explain why she had essentially uninvited him, and he had to know that she would be thorough in her reasoning.

"Yeah, she, uh…she had a bit of a fall. Nothing too serious, but they want to keep her overnight," Ryan lied. "I'm closest, so it's easy for me to swing by and grab her a change of clothes, make sure all her doors are locked, that sort of thing."

"Well, I hope she feels better soon," Jeanine said with a note of dismissal. The others offered their best wishes for Ryan's aunt as well, their words effectively ushering him away.

"Thanks for that," Sasha whispered to Jeanine.

"No problem. I wouldn't want my ex at a celebratory dinner like this, either," she whispered back.

"Who're we waiting on?" Allison from the main research team asked, looking around.

"I kind of invited some of the guys from sports," Sasha mentioned.

"Okay, but this dinner is not about talking shop," Jeanine reminded her. "It's about celebrating the work you've already done."

There was a bit of commotion down the hall, and the women collectively turned to see the guys from sports approaching, but there was one too many of them. They were crowded around Fox, who was politely smiling and dodging their questions about the contract rumors, explaining that he hadn't been in touch with his agent and anything like that would go through his agent and manager first. His eyes locked on Sasha, and her pulse ticked up. He looked too good. Tattoos on full display. Looking like a total badass. He didn't have the bleached blonde with him, so that was something. If he was here to yell at her, she was in no kind of mood.

"Fox," she managed to croak as her friends' and colleagues' eyes darted back and forth between them. "Congrats on the game earlier. You were amazing. Sorry we couldn't talk after. You were clearly busy, and I had to get back."

"Uh...thanks, Sash. Could we, uh... Do you think I could talk with you for a minute? Privately...?"

"Um..." Sasha glanced around.

"If this is the whole party," Jeanine stepped in, "we can call ahead and let them know we're on our way. There, uh...there might be a bit of a wait with a party of this size, so take as long as you need."

Sasha nodded and led Fox through the knot of her coworkers in search of an empty room where he could say his piece. She was a little scared, thinking that maybe that he wanted to let her know that he was moving out. That he'd be by to pick up his stuff the next day, and that living together had been a bad idea. Or worse, he was sleeping with the blonde. She didn't want to go back to where they'd been before, but she'd rather have his friendship than nothing. It would kill her, but she could do it.

Finally, she found an abandoned conference room and pulled him inside.

"I'm sorry…" he said immediately, "for hanging up on you like I did…when you said… I wasn't sure…I was mad and hurt and…I didn't know what to— And fuck, that groupie. It wasn't what it looked like."

"I shouldn't have just…blurted it out like that, and especially after the way I behaved toward you for the photo thing…and I get it if you don't love me back," she interrupted, looking down at the coat she had draped over her clasped hands. "I get it. I hurt you."

"Of course I love you," he said quickly, startling her into silence. "Fuck, I'm bad at this. That's…what I should have said…instead of hanging up. I…I should have said it…much sooner— probably during that first night… But you'd just broken up with Ryan, and you said—"

Her head snapped up. What did he just say? "I...I know what I said, and I *thought* it's what I wanted, but...everything with you has been...it feels right."

Fox took her hand. "Coach Tremblay said they're going to get me a proper contract. It meant the world to me that you were there. I hated that I couldn't call you and talk to you about everything. Dax and my parents were excited for me, but...it wasn't the same as when *you* get excited for me. When *you* get excited for me, it becomes real... I can finally believe it. And no one had a sign."

Sasha leaned into him. "You're going to get a contract from the team?" she asked in a quietly playful tone. Her fingers reached toward where his hand rested on the back of one of the conference room chairs. She lightly touched the back of his hand and trailed her fingers up his arm as she moved closer to him.

"Uh-huh," he answered, the reply almost a grunt as his head bent toward hers.

"Congratulations," she whispered, and then she turned her face just enough to meet his kiss. The first kiss was soft, a mutual apology.

The second was more greedy. She clutched his arm with one hand as the other slid up to clasp the back of his head. She felt his hands lock on her

waist as he pulled her against him. Then they slid to
embrace her tightly, and he lifted her just off her
feet, their lips disconnecting as he gave her a small
spin of celebration, both of them laughing.

"We should get back," she murmured
without conviction as his lips sought the warm spot
where her ear and the edge of her jaw created a little
hollow. "I can't blow off dinner with them when
they've gone to so much trouble..." she said
breathily. His lips were working their way down
her neck, and his hands had drifted down from the
small of her back to cup and squeeze her buttocks.
"But you can come, too," she added as his hands
drifted farther down the backs of her thighs toward
the hem of her skirt. "We can sit together." Her
hands slid down his torso, feeling for the muscles
she knew lay beneath the thin layer of cotton. Her
palm skimmed over his waistband as she sought
and stroked his cock over his clothing, smiling at his
low growl.

"Fine," he conceded, giving her ass a final
squeeze. "No appetizers, eat fast, and we can either
order dessert to go or see what's in the freezer at
home," he suggested.

They reluctantly pulled away from one
another, but Sasha took his hand as they headed
back to where her coworkers were waiting for them.

"All set on the reservation?" she asked, ignoring the inquisitive gazes that dropped to where her hand was linked with Fox's. Not to mention the flush she was sure was evident in her cheeks.

"Uh, yeah. They have one of their event rooms available, but it'll take a while to get it set up for us," Jeanine explained. "We can head over whenever, though, and just wait at the bar. We were starting to arrange carpools to save on gas…"

"I'll ride with Fox and meet you there, all right?" Sasha said, giving his hand a squeeze.

"Perfect," Jeanine said before anyone else could comment. "We were trying to figure out how to fit everyone into my SUV and Natalie's van without having to take out her kids' car seats. If you two go separately, the seats can stay put."

"Well…let's go, then," Sasha said, waving her arm to usher everyone in the direction of the elevators.

When they reached the parking garage, the group split up.

"Come on," Sasha insisted, pulling Fox toward a dark corner of the lot. "I'm parked over this way."

"We can take my car," Fox offered. "I got a spot right near the entrance."

"Actually…" Sasha said, biting her lip and dropping her voice, even though she knew they were out of anyone else's hearing range. "I had a little thought about that 'Never Have I Ever' list from the other night…"

"Oh, did you?" he asked with a broad grin that sent a delicious shiver through her belly.

She felt the warmth of him behind her, closer than he'd been moments before. They were standing in front of her car — it was a four-door sedan, but had plenty of leg and headroom, in addition to soft leather seats.

"I think I'm going to like this boyfriend-girlfriend arrangement," he said with a low rumble in his voice. Fox turned her around and pinned to the side of the car, his hips impatiently pressing against hers, as he picked up where he'd left off. He kissed her throat, his hands trailing up under her suit jacket and skimming over her blouse to press against her firm breasts.

"You know…car sex usually takes place *in* the car," she teased, one hand stroking his cock while the other untucked his shirt from his pants. "Let's get in."

He sighed as he pulled away. It took a little maneuvering — the people next to her passenger side had parked a little close — but he was soon seated in a reclining position in her passenger seat while she lifted her skirt up over her thighs so the bulk of the fabric sat on her hips. The tops of her nylon stockings reached to her mid-thigh, and she was sure her silky black panties would be seen easily if anyone happened by. She ducked her head and climbed into the car, straddling Fox and resting her ass on his knees as she settled herself in enough to close the door behind her.

"Now I remember why car sex never held a lot of appeal for me," he joked as she inadvertently smacked him in the face with the sleeve of her suit jacket while taking it off. She threw it onto the driver's seat and tugged her skirt up a little higher, then she leaned forward to help Fox free himself from his boxers.

"I think you forgot something," he said, running a finger along the seam of her panties before rubbing at her damp cleft. "Also, I know that friend of yours said that there was going to be a bit of a wait, but I think they'll notice if we show up so much later than they do."

"Oh," Sasha said as she ran her fingers up and down his pulsing erection. "I'm glad to hear you don't plan to rush things. Besides…I did tell them I wanted to ride you and then meet them there."

Planting her knees firmly into the leather on either side of his hips, Sasha took hold of his cock and guided him into her, tugging aside the crotch of her panties and lowering herself onto him slowly, pausing to get a feel for how they fit together in this new position with such cramped quarters.

"Actually," Fox said, swallowing with difficulty as his breathing became ragged, "I believe you said you wanted to ride *with* me."

"Ah," she sighed as she adjusted her position and he slid a little deeper. *Oh, yes.* "Pesky preposition. Chalk it up to being a typo." Her breathing became uneven, and she could feel him twitch inside her.

"You know," he said, "I had a dream like this last night. Well, we were in the shower, not a car—"

Sasha rocked her hips to a steady rhythm and he leaned his head back with a low groan and a forceful thrust into her. "But you…you were riding me like this," he continued.

She settled her hands on his shoulders, her forearms braced against his chest as she rotated her hips and tried to maximize the friction between them. "And did you like it? In your dream, I mean." She bit her lip.

His hands slid along her thighs to her hips, loosening her blouse from the waist of her skirt before sliding to her buttocks and taking a firm hold to raise her off him momentarily and then re-sheathe himself in her. "Yes," he assured her as she stifled a moan. "But I like the reality better."

"We'll have to…try this…in the shower…sometime then…for the sake of…comparison," she panted.

His shoulders didn't give her the leverage she longed for so she reached above her head and braced herself against the ceiling, groaning at the additional pressure she was able to utilize as she sought friction.

Fox was busy fiddling with the buttons on her blouse, trying not to lose any in his haste to compare the silkiness of her skin to the silk of her shirt. The seat was in a reclining position, but he fought to sit up, bracing himself on the console between the two front seats. She cried out as he pulled the cups of her bra down and seized the supple flesh of her breasts, pulling one to his mouth and rubbing the nipple of the other with the pad of his thumb. It was effective, but not what she needed most.

She took his hand from her breast and drew it down between her legs, guiding his fingers as he started massaging the sensitive button just above where they were joined. Her body's response was

immediate and intense. With nothing to hold on to
on the ceiling, she leaned back and rested her hands
on his rigid thighs, all of the muscles from her neck
down convulsing as her release washed through
her.

His hands reached for her wrists, grasping
them and pulling her toward him so that they both
fell against the reclining seat, her breasts crushed
against his chest. "You're coming…with me…next
time," he told her as he took firm hold of her
buttocks and guided her, jerking his hips and
plunging inside. Stroke, retreat, stroke, retreat. She
clasped his shoulders and leaned her forehead to
his, locking eyes with him as his pace increased and
the muscles in her legs began to ache as she melted
from the inside out. When he jerked to a stop, she
commanded her thighs to clench and hold him tight
within, so she could savor the synchronized pulsing
as he came deep within her with a roar.

"I love you," she whispered.

"I love you, too," he breathed against her
lips, before tasting them and seeking to do the same
with her tongue.

She wanted to stay and doze against him, but
as the sweat cooled on her limbs, she became
increasingly aware of how exposed they were.
"We're going to be more than just fashionably late if

we don't leave soon," she remarked.

"Well…you were the mastermind of getting us into this particular position…do you have any idea how to get back out of it?" he asked. "I mean…am I supposed to toss you over the arm rest and into the driver's seat…?"

They both turned their heads to look at the obstacles around them and laughed.

"Now I'm thinking we should've just done it in the backseat," she responded, reaching down to tuck her breasts back into her bra and re-button her blouse.

"We'll do that one on the way home."

"You're incorrigible."

He grinned. "If that means horny and in love with my girlfriend, then yes."

Epilogue

Two more exams, and Sasha was done with classes and would have her master's degree. She had been studying relentlessly, though Fox made sure she took breaks every now and then and helped take her mind off of the material long enough to actually relax.

She was able to let herself relax because her internship was over and the photo shoots for Echo's premier collection were complete, so all she had to worry about for the time being were her classes.

The station had offered her a contract, but after her story was featured on the website for a national syndicate, she had received a few other job offers as well. Sasha was weighing her options, waiting until she had matriculated and could breathe freely before making her final decision.

She was leaning toward one of the weekly newsmagazine programs headquartered just a few blocks from the arena where she currently sat while watching Fox play and trying to keep her hands off her textbooks.

"How're you holding up?" Echo asked as she moved to the front of the private box and took a seat beside Sasha.

"How many minutes left in the period?" Sasha asked. "My fingers are itching for intermission so I won't feel guilty about double-checking those quotes I need to memorize."

Echo chuckled. "When's graduation day?"

"The ceremony is next Thursday night—one of the best things about graduating during the winter session is that the graduation ceremony is low-key," Sasha explained.

"Not interested in making a big show of it?"

"There are other ways I'd rather celebrate. It's an off-night for Fox, and the team won't be traveling again until a few days before Christmas, so he'll be able to make it."

"And your parents?"

Sasha shrugged. "Mom's coming. And Dad…Well, my dad couldn't be happier about me and Fox being together, so he'll be there."

"I take it you're not going to stay behind and visit with your parents over Christmas."

Sasha grinned. "Nope. I'm very much looking forward to spending a quiet Christmas on the road with Fox and the team. I mean…I'm sorry he has to play an away game on Christmas, 'cause it means we won't get to spend any of the holiday with *your* family," Sasha quickly backtracked. "But as far as my own family is concerned, a trip to the East Coast is the best Christmas gift Fox could get me."

"Well, we'll be having a New Year's Eve party at Bryce and Tami's place, so as long as you can make it to that, the Coulters will be pacified." Echo shrugged. "And the family dinner tonight, of course."

"That's why I need to cram so much studying in during the next intermission," Sasha explained. "I promised Fox that I'd put the books away for at least twelve hours, starting with the end of the game."

"Sounds like a good plan to me." Echo patted her arm. "And for the record, I'm glad you guys are together."

The buzzer sounded, and Sasha had her book back in her lap, the spine cracked, before Fox and his teammates had finished their trek down the tunnel to the locker room.

***

Fox kissed Sasha's shoulder. This was where he always wanted to be. He had a temporary contract in place for the rest of the season just two weeks after being called up, but his agent and manager had been working with the team's legal representatives and owners to negotiate something more long-term.

Henri was proving to be an effective first-choice goalie, but as the season wore on, he was having a harder and harder time completing a string of starts, even when there were two or three days between games.

Fox had made an impression in his first few starts, but a couple of losses, one of which he was reluctant to count since he'd been swapped in for Henri after the other goalie had let four pucks past him, had brought his numbers back to a steady average. That loss to the Rajun Cajuns had been brutal. Ransom Cox had almost gotten one past him. Shit, that guy was fast.

There had been a number of injuries among the team's players. Martin was still recovering from a bad concussion, and Gerry had missed a few weeks after breaking a finger. The younger players that had been called up at the beginning of the season were doing okay but not great, so even though the season was young, the chances of the Brawlers making the playoffs this year were slim.

The team was doing what it could to prepare for the next season, intending to build the skills and discipline of the young blood so they'd be a coordinated unit for the following year. Coach Tremblay was pleased with Fox's level of discipline and hoped he would prove effective in instilling it into the other players on the team.

"Talent is necessary, but it is easily undermined without the patience and dedication that develop and direct it." Tremblay had repeatedly told the team this at many practices or after games when someone went for the glory shot instead of the smart one.

When Fox told Sasha what the coach had said, she wasn't surprised. "You've always doubted your talents," she said, wiggling her naked back against his chest. She pulled his hand from where it pressed against the flat of her stomach up to her lips so she could press a kiss to his knuckles. "That doubt is why you asked *me* to take shots on you when we were kids. It didn't matter who you were facing off with, you needed to drill every shot into your muscle memory."

His hand drifted to her breast and then trailed down past its former spot on her belly, as his cock twitched against her ass.

"I know of something else that could do with some drilling to reinforce…muscle memory." He murmured in her ear, his fingers sliding between her legs.

She laughed at his terrible double entendre but widened her thighs in invitation, hitching her leg over his and reaching back to clutch the thick muscles of his quads as he slid into her and she arched against him.

"Coulter," Coach Tremblay called for him from the main locker room. Fox dragged his mind away from the memory of last night.

"Yeah, Coach?" he called back, turning off the water in front of him and grabbing a towel to wrap around his waist so he could see what Tremblay wanted.

"PR guys want you on the stage for the post-game press conference. They know about your new contract, so be prepared for questions about that, too."

"I've got family waiting on me in the box," he told his coach, hoping it would be enough to get him out of the press conference. "I'm pretty sure my parents have reservations."

"Then we'll make it quick," Tremblay said without any sympathy.

Fox fought the urge to fidget through the reporters' questions as he watched the clock advancing and wished they would wrap it up already so he could find Sasha and the others. He wanted to get the family dinner over with so he and Sasha could get home. She'd promised she'd give the studying a rest for a couple of days. And he had very specific plans for how he wanted to use the time with her.

He thought for a brief moment that he might successfully escape without any questions about his new contract or his role on the team, but as luck would have it, the last reporter to be acknowledged touched on just that.

"Congratulations on your contract," the reporter began, "and given that this is already being referred to as a 'team building' year, is there anything you would like to see change in relation to your position in goal? Your numbers in some areas are, in fact, better than your fellow goalie's. Is there a chance you might swap positions on the bench by the end of the year?"

Sasha must have come looking for him because he spotted her standing in the doorway to the pressroom. She had an amused smile on her face and crossed her arms over her chest as she too waited for his answer.

"Well...I've worked for a long time to get to where I am. There were plenty of times in the last few years when I doubted that I would ever have what I've got now...so I'm not complaining about any of it. I'll do what the team needs me to do, and I'll do it as well as I can, just like pretty much every other guy out there on that ice does every game. Things come up during the season. Unfortunately, we've had some guys get hurt, and so sometimes the rest of us have to step up and do more. But I'm where I want to be. I'm on a team I'm happy with, I'm getting to be in goal, and I'm excited to see what the future holds."

Sasha grinned from the doorway, and he could see her giving him a slow clap. He bit the inside of his cheek to keep from laughing.

"Fox, just one more question," a blonde reporter on the right spoke up.

"Sure, go ahead." His eyes were still on Sasha.

"Have you ever noticed the striking resemblance between you and your opponent today? The Winger, Ransom Cox?"

"No, I didn't." He stroked his head. "Sorry, I was too busy trying to keep the guy from scoring."

She nodded, putting the pen cap to her mouth. "Well, I understand. But without the pads, he could be a long-lost Coulter."

"I'm sorry. I don't know anything about the guy, other than he's fast." Fox stood. "Now, if you'll all excuse me, I have my girlfriend to kiss." He didn't wait to be dismissed, just went straight for Sasha and pulled her into his arms. "Come on, oh love of my life, let's go eat. The sooner we do that, the sooner I can have you naked."

Sasha laughed. "Now, who's incorrigible?"

About Nana Malone

USA Today Bestselling Author, Nana Malone's love of all things romance and adventure started with a tattered romantic suspense she borrowed from her cousin on a sultry summer afternoon in Ghana at a precocious thirteen. She's been in love with kick butt heroines ever since.

With her overactive imagination, and channeling her inner Buffy, it was only a matter a time before she started creating her own characters. Waiting for her chance at a job as a ninja assassin, Nana, meantime works out her drama, passion and sass with fictional characters every bit as sassy and kick butt as she thinks she is.

Until that ninja job comes through, you'll find Nana working hard on additional books for her series as well as other fun, sassy romances for characters that won't leave her alone. And if she's not working or hiding in the closet reading, she's acting out scenes for her husband, daughter and puppy in sunny San Diego.

Made in the USA
San Bernardino, CA
17 September 2017